"WHAT DO WE DO ABOUT US, LUCY?" SCOTT ASKED. "What do you want?"

"Me?" She shrugged. "I don't know," she said, trembling beneath the intensity of his gaze. She did know, but did she dare confess it to him! "I suppose I want what every woman wants," she answered vaguely.

He arched a brow. "Most women want a home. Husband, family, love, the whole nine yards. Is that what you want?"

She sighed. "I used to. But that dream died fifteen years ago. I told myself I had no choice but to accept it and go on."

He surprised her by reaching for her hand and slipping it inside his shirt to press against his chest. "Feel that?" he said. "My heart's still beating. I'm very much alive."

Lucy could feel her own heart thrumming in time with his. She closed her eyes, thinking, *If only things had not turned out the way they had. If only . . .*

"Look at me, Lucy," he said. She opened her eyes. His face was close, his expression full of fire. "I never got over you. . . ."

WHAT ARE *LOVESWEPT* ROMANCES?

They are stories of true romance and touching emotion. We believe those two very important ingredients are constants in our highly sensual and very believable stories in the LOVE-SWEPT line. Our goal is to give you, the reader, stories of consistently high quality that may sometimes make you laugh, sometimes make you cry, but are always fresh and creative and contain many delightful surprises within their pages.

Most romance fans read an enormous number of books. Those they truly love, they keep. Others may be traded with friends and soon forgotten. We hope that each LOVESWEPT romance will be a treasure—a "keeper." We will always try to publish

LOVE STORIES YOU'LL NEVER FORGET
BY AUTHORS YOU'LL ALWAYS REMEMBER

The Editors

Loveswept® 795

BELATED BRIDE

CHARLOTTE HUGHES

BANTAM BOOKS
NEW YORK · TORONTO · LONDON · SYDNEY · AUCKLAND

BELATED BRIDE

A Bantam Book / July 1996

ISBN 0-553-44523-5

Published simultaneously in the United States and Canada

Bantam Books are published by Bantam Books, a division of Bantam Dou-
bleday Dell Publishing Group, Inc. Its trademark, consisting of the words
"Bantam Books" and the portrayal of a rooster, is Registered in U.S. Patent
and Trademark Office and in other countries. Marca Registrada. Bantam
Books, 1540 Broadway, New York, New York 10036.

PRINTED IN THE UNITED STATES OF AMERICA

OPM   0 9 8 7 6 5 4 3 2 1

ACKNOWLEDGMENT

Many thanks to pilot Skip Shelton for explaining how one goes about crashing a perfectly fine single-engine Cessna 182.

PROLOGUE

Shade Tree, Florida—July 1980

The fog lifted by degrees, from a heavy gray shroud that cloaked his brain and left him feeling groggy and closed off from the rest of the world to something less burdensome and, at times, wispy.

He was aware of voices, his father's loud and booming, snapping orders here and there, then a softer voice that somehow instilled calm, assured him everything was going to be okay. How long he lay in this listless, dreamlike state, he couldn't say.

Then one day, seventeen-year-old Scott Bufford simply woke up.

"Heavenly days, McGee, he's awake!" a woman said, obviously a nurse, for she was dressed in white. "Mr. Bufford, your son is awake! I'm going to alert his doctor." She hurried out of the room.

Aubrey Bufford was a hulking figure of a man who moved slowly under normal circumstances, mainly because there was no need for him to race about. He was rich, so people did his running for him. This day, though, he literally leapt from the recliner in which he'd been dozing and was at his son's hospital bed in a flash.

"Scott, you're awake. You gave me the scare of my life. Your poor mother is beside herself. Why, the doctor has been out at the house almost daily for a month now, treating her migraines."

A month? Scott Bufford tried to lift his head, but the pain was excruciating, as though someone had used a band saw along the back of his skull. He glanced down at his body and saw that he was swathed in bandages.

"Where am I?" He could barely form the words because his face and jaw were immobile from what he assumed were more bandages.

"Shade Tree General Hospital," Aubrey said. "You had a car accident. Don't you remember? A drunk driver hit you head-on. He died instantly." He said it gleefully.

Scott tried to remember back before the fog had closed in. Slowly, it came back to him, a big blue Buick jumping the median and heading straight for them. Panic seized him.

"Lucy?" he said.

"She's fine, son. Because you swerved the car to the right, she managed to escape serious injury. A few broken bones, but nothing that won't heal. She has already left the hospital."

"What about . . . the baby?"

Aubrey took one of his son's hands. "The baby didn't make it, Scott. It was stillborn."

The boy in the bed seemed to crumble. Tears filled his eyes. He looked away for a moment. "How badly . . . am I . . . hurt?"

"Hard to say, son. We'd just about given up on you ever coming out of that coma." He paused. "Your face got the brunt of it, I'm afraid, but don't let that worry you none. I flew in the best plastic surgeons money can buy. They've been working on that puss of yours since day one. Lord, boy, by the time they get finished, you won't be able to beat the girls off with a stick.

"As for what else is wrong with you, they performed surgery on you in the beginning to take care of the internal stuff. You've got your share of broken bones and some kind of spinal injury, although the spinal column itself is not fractured, thank goodness. The fact that you're awake and know who you are means a helluva lot."

"Has Lucy been to see me?" Scott asked at last.

Aubrey sighed and wiped his brow, despite the fact that it was more than comfortable in the room. Outside, the day was hot and muggy. "Lucy left town, Scott. I really didn't want to have to break the news to you so soon after what you've been through."

Left town? Scott almost raised himself up this time. "You mean she left Shade Tree?"

"Settle down now," his father said, pushing the boy gently to his pillow.

Scott looked and felt frantic. Lucy gone? "Where?"

"I don't know," Aubrey said. He paused. "You might as well know the truth. She hit me up for a lot of money. I think she saw this as an opportunity to get out of town and away from that white-trash family of hers once and for all. Not that I blame her. Everybody knows what a worthless drunk her daddy is. And mean to boot. Why, I've heard tales . . ."

Scott wasn't listening. The thought that Lucy Odum, *his Lucy*, would desert him while he lay near death was more than he could stand. They were to have been married before the end of the summer, once they'd both turned eighteen and didn't need a parent's signature. They had been looking forward to the birth of their baby.

Scott closed his eyes, wishing now he'd gone ahead and died. Inside, where it counted, he felt as though he already had.

ONE

Shade Tree, Florida—January 1996

Lucy Odum followed the group of mourners from the alcove of the church to the small cemetery out back. The day was cold and bleak, the air heavy with mist.

A perfect day for her father's funeral.

The coffin was metal and cheap-looking. Lucy knew her mother had bought the entire funeral package for less than two thousand dollars and would make monthly payments on it for a long time to come. The plot where Darnel Odum was about to be laid was free because his wife had attended Faith Baptist Church all her life.

Lucy glanced at her mother to see how she was holding up, and some part of her was thankful to find the woman dry-eyed. Now in her early fifties, Loretta Odum looked older than her years. She had let herself go. Her clothes were dowdy, her shoes badly scuffed, and her once-pretty face as plump as an overstuffed throw pillow.

Lucy felt someone tug her coat sleeve. Her fifteen-year-old daughter leaned close. "I'm cold, Mom."

"I know, honey," Lucy whispered back, praying they wouldn't all get sick standing in the elements. The otherwise modest temperature had plunged during the night, and their unlined cotton twill trench coats simply weren't warm enough. "Fasten your top button," she told Kelly. "This shouldn't take long."

"The Lord is my shepherd . . ."

Lucy stood there feeling emotionally numb as they committed her father's body to the earth. A gust of wind whipped her light brown hair about her face. She took her mother's hand and held it. Reverend Snodgrass had aged drastically in the time she had been gone. Too many sickbeds and funerals, she supposed. She remembered the time he'd visited the house, tried to get Darnel to start attending church. Her father had threatened to shoot him on sight if he ever set foot on his property again.

"And I shall dwell in the house of the Lord forever. Amen."

Fat chance of that, Lucy thought.

Lucy had not been home in fifteen years. Although her mother had been quite particular at one time, the house now looked shabby. As she parked in the driveway behind her mother's battered station wagon, she sensed her daughter was equally disappointed.

"Am I supposed to call her Grandma?" the girl asked.

"I know it'll be awkward at first, but you'll get used to it."

The mist had turned to rain. Lucy and Kelly climbed from the car and hurried to the house, where a church member stood at the door welcoming guests. "You must be Loretta's daughter," he said, giving her hand a hearty shake. "And this pretty young thing is Kelly. Food's in the kitchen."

Lucy wondered how the man knew who they were. With the exception of birthday and Christmas cards that bore no return address, she had not contacted or visited her mother even once during the entire fifteen years she'd been gone. Only two days before, Lucy had received a phone call at the hospital where she worked from the funeral director, telling her that her father had succumbed to cirrhosis of the liver. She hadn't even known he was sick.

The booze had finally gotten to him.

The house was warm inside, the small kitchen filled with people wearing their Sunday best. The counters and Formica table held enough food for the entire town of Shade Tree. "Grab something to eat," Lucy whispered to Kelly. "I want to check on Grandma."

Lucy hurried down the hall to her mother's room and knocked softly. She heard a muffled sound and went inside. The bedroom was dim. Her mother lay on her side, having kicked off her shoes.

"Did you get something to eat, dear?" she asked Lucy. "I can't believe how thin you are. I'll bet you're one of those women who live off salads."

"I'll grab something later," Lucy said. She walked over to the bed and sat down, then switched on the lamp so she could get a better look at her mother. "Are you okay?"

"Oh, yes, I'm better now. I guess the last few days took their toll on me. Actually, the last few months were pretty bad, with your father so sick and all. He didn't go into the hospital until the very end. Said he wanted to die right here in his own bed. It all caught up with me, I reckon."

Lucy wasn't at all surprised her father had chosen to spend his remaining days at home, where his wife would be forced to care for him around-the-clock instead of a team of health professionals. No wonder her mother looked so haggard.

Lucy noted the prescription bottles on the night table and reached for them. "What's all this?" She picked one up.

"Now, Lucy," her mother said on a chuckle. "You're a nurse, I'm sure you'll figure it out. But I'm so glad to see you and Kelly. Let's not talk about that now."

Lucy glanced at her. "How'd you know I was a nurse?"

"I hired someone to find you, a couple of months ago when your father took a turn for the worse. It cost me my whole savings, but it was worth it. Kelly's beautiful. Why, she's the spit and image of her father. Speaking of which—"

"I don't want to talk about Scott right now either, Mother. How long have you been a diabetic?"

"Oh, gosh, for years. It's no big deal," Loretta said, waving the whole thing aside. "My mother was a diabetic and *her* mother was one. It's only natural that I should have it."

"Do you have to take insulin?"

"Only rarely. My medication seems to do the trick, thank goodness. Sometimes, though, when I get busy or forget to eat, it backfires on me."

"Are you able to work?" Lucy knew the work at the orange juice plant where her mother had been employed more than twenty-five years could be grueling.

"Oh, yes, I do okay. They finally gave me a desk job a couple of years back, so it's not so bad."

Lucy sat on the bed and took her mother's hand. "You know what aggravates this disease," she said flatly.

"Of course I do. I'm fat. And my doctor rubs my nose in that fact every time I go in for a checkup."

"Now that Darnel's gone, you'll have more time for yourself."

Loretta sighed heavily. "I don't know, Lucy. I guess I'm just not motivated."

"What if it becomes a matter of life and death?" Lucy asked gently. Her mother shrugged and shook her head sadly. Lucy then realized her mother had spent so many years caring for her husband that she didn't have the first clue how to take care of herself.

Lucy was no closer to understanding why her mother had put up with Darnel Odum than she had been fifteen years earlier. Of course, there were textbook answers like codependency and battered women's syndrome, but those words weren't being tossed around much when Lucy was seventeen and determined to flee with her baby. Wealthy Aubrey Bufford had simply made her escape a reality.

"Mom, I want you to come back to Atlanta with Kelly and me," Lucy said at last. "I can't leave you like this."

Loretta looked stunned. "I can't just pick up and leave Shade Tree," she said. "This is where I was born and raised, where my church and my friends are. Besides, I wouldn't last five minutes in a big city."

Lucy suspected it was true, although she argued with her mother for the next fifteen minutes before giving up. Finally, she decided to check on Kelly. She found her at the dining room table playing gin rummy with the man who'd welcomed them at the door.

Lucy saw that the church ladies were cleaning up. "I just want to grab something for my mother," she said.

A gray-haired woman at the sink turned and smiled. "It's all taken care of. I prepared a plate for you *and* Loretta. It's sitting on the stove there."

Lucy lifted the aluminum foil on one of the plates and frowned at what she saw. Thick ham slices oozed glaze. It ran into double helpings of scalloped potatoes, and collard greens that were seasoned with salt pork. Beside that were several slices of fried green tomatoes and a large hunk of corn bread. Oh, Lord, she thought. If this didn't kill her mother, nothing would.

"Is something wrong?" one of the ladies asked.

Lucy smiled brightly. "Oh, no, everything's fine. I was just trying to decide what my mother might like to drink."

"I've already poured her a glass of iced tea."

Lucy carried the plate and glass down the hall to her mother's room. "I brought you something to eat," she said, handing her the plate of food, "but I may as well tell you, after tonight you're finished with fried food and gravies and such. I'm going to the grocery store tomorrow for healthy stuff."

Loretta did not look thrilled at the prospect.

Once Lucy had seen the last of the guests out, she showed Kelly the bedroom in which they would sleep. "This was my room before I moved away," she said, noting everything was much the same save for the dust. "I hope you don't mind sharing. The house has only two bedrooms."

Kelly was only too happy to go to bed. She slipped into her nightgown and crawled beneath the covers. She yawned wide. "Are you sorry you left this place?"

Lucy stood there for a moment, wondering how to respond. It seemed so long ago, another lifetime actually, that she'd gazed down at a comatose Scott Bufford.

She could still remember the look of devastation on his father's face when a nurse had reluctantly rolled her into Scott's room after she'd threatened to go on her own.

"They don't expect him to live through the day," Aubrey Bufford had said, his voice as cold as a December wind. "They've even asked me to pull his life support. I want this time alone with my son."

Lucy had felt as though she were living a nightmare. Her entire left arm was in a heavy cast, and she was literally taped from the waist up. Giving birth had been no small feat, she'd discovered, and because she'd wanted so desperately to nurse her baby, she'd foregone painkillers. "I'm not going to leave him," she said adamantly.

"Listen to me," Aubrey said, grabbing her good arm. His eyes were angry slits. "This time tomorrow I'll be making funeral arrangements for my boy. I don't want to have to look at your face one more minute than I have to. I told Scott what you were, but he refused to listen to me. I'll even pay you to leave town. You'll have enough money to get away from your old man once and for all. You'll be able to get some sort of education. You have no choice, Lucy. If you don't go, I'll have the baby taken away from you."

That last sentence had made her decision for her. "But what if he lives? What if by some miracle he—"

"You don't believe in miracles any more than I do." When she continued to hedge, he gave an awful sneer. "How about I send you his obituary notice when it's over."

Lucy had opted to run rather than stay behind and risk losing her child. At the time, it felt like the right decision, the *only* decision for a frightened seventeen-year-old. Now, at thirty-two, she felt she could hold her own with the likes of Aubrey Bufford.

"Mom, are you even listening to me?" Kelly said.

Suddenly realizing her daughter was speaking to her, Lucy blinked. "I'm sorry, baby, what did you say?"

"I wanted to know if we could visit my father's grave while we're here."

Lucy hesitated. She knew she'd been unfair to her daughter by lying about her relationship with Kelly's father. Because she worried that Kelly might think badly of her for having a baby out of wedlock, she had made up a story that she and Scott had been married briefly before he was killed in a car accident. Kelly obviously sensed it was painful for her to talk about him, because she seldom pushed for more answers than Lucy wanted to give.

"Of course we can, honey," she said at last.

She dropped a quick kiss on her daughter's forehead and slipped from the room, making her way in her stocking feet to the living room. It was quiet now with everybody gone. Peaceful. It had never been that way when Darnel was living. She studied the room. The carpet was threadbare, the furniture sagged, and the wall paint all washed out. She sat in the recliner that had been her father's and wondered what to do next.

Scott Bufford's grave was nowhere to be found. Lucy had searched the cemetery for more than an hour, and although she'd stumbled over several generations of Buffords, including Scott's father, who'd passed away the year before, Scott's final resting place was simply not there.

Lucy tried to remember exactly what the obituary had said. *"Seventeen-year-old Scott Bufford died today from injuries sustained in a car accident on July 3, 1980. He will be buried at Shady Gardens after a private service. Survivors include . . ."*

It didn't make sense. Could he have been cremated instead, she wondered?

Lucy didn't have time to search further, since she was supposed to be at the grocery store. She was more than a little puzzled when she climbed into her car and drove away.

She would call the business office later and learn what she could.

It was funny, Lucy thought later that night as she and Kelly prepared for bed. Returning to Shade Tree hadn't been as hard as she'd feared it would be. With Aubrey Bufford and Darnel gone, she wasn't afraid anymore of the past. Somehow being home again made her feel closer to Scott, even though she hadn't been able to locate his grave. She decided to ask Kelly the question she'd been mulling over all day. "What would you say to moving to Shade Tree for a while? Grandma really needs us."

Two weeks later, Lucy and Kelly arrived in Shade Tree pulling a small trailer containing all their belongings. Loretta, who'd been thrilled from the beginning, was beside herself with joy and called several men from church to help unload the trailer. With their help, they finished in record time, storing most of the items in the small detached garage and carrying the rest inside the house.

"Have you been eating right?" Lucy asked her mother once they were alone.

"Of course, dear."

But when Lucy checked the refrigerator and freezer, she saw that Loretta had barely touched the groceries she'd bought. On top of that, it looked like an entire platoon of maids had descended on the house, and it smelled cleaner than any hospital Lucy had worked in. Although she was perturbed, she decided not to say anything for the moment.

Loretta, in her excitement to have them there, ended up having to pop a piece of hard candy and lie down for a few minutes when her blood sugar level dropped. Lucy ordered her to remain in bed while she drove into town and returned the rented trailer.

Kelly was unpacking her suitcase and putting her clothes away in the room they shared, when Lucy came home. "How's Grandma?"

"I've checked on her a couple of times. She seems okay," Kelly said.

"I think I'll have a look." Her mother was in bed, reading her Bible. "You've been cleaning this place the entire time I've been gone, haven't you?" Lucy said disapprovingly. "No wonder you're exhausted."

"I didn't want you to come back to a dirty house. I used to be so particular; I'm afraid I let everything go when your father got so sick."

Lucy sat on the edge of the bed. "Right now I'm more concerned with getting you healthy than having the house sparkle." Once Loretta promised to take it easier, she changed the subject. "Have I received any mail?" Lucy had sent her résumé to as many places as she could think of during the past two weeks, hoping she might not have to wait too long before finding another job. She hated to dip into her savings account any more than was necessary.

"I left the mail on the mantel in the living room," Loretta told her.

"I want to take a look at it. Try to rest now, okay? I'll cook dinner tonight."

Lucy made her way out of the room, down the narrow hall, and into the living room, where she found a short stack of mail addressed to her. For the next fifteen minutes, she sifted through it.

The hospital wasn't hiring, but they would be happy to hold on to her application in case there was an opening. The small clinic had hired someone the day before they received her résumé, and they were very sorry they couldn't help her. Once again, they would keep her application on file. The only job that looked promising was one with the nursing home on the edge of town. They were interviewing RNs presently and invited her to call at her earliest convenience.

Lucy was dressed and ready by seven-thirty on Monday. Her appointment was for nine o'clock, but first she had to register Kelly in school. The drive to Shade Tree High School was a silent one.

"What's wrong, Kel?" she asked her daughter.

"I'm nervous. I wish we'd never come here."

"We talked about it, and you promised you'd give the place a chance."

"Mom, these people are so different from the people I knew in Atlanta."

"Well, maybe you'll appear more sophisticated to them, having lived in the big city, and all."

"You think so?" Kelly seemed to ponder it. When Lucy left the school some thirty minutes later, her daughter seemed calmer.

Restful Valley was located on the other side of town, a sprawling one-story building surrounded by a perfectly manicured lawn. Lucy met with the personnel director, Alice Bloom, and the two hit it off right away.

"Your résumé is impressive, as were your references," Alice said. "Eight years with one of the best hospitals in Atlanta. I see you've worked in every area from trauma to labor and delivery."

"It was good experience for me," Lucy said. "I also spent a lot of time in geriatrics, which I think would be helpful here."

"We'd love to have you join our crew," Alice said. "Unfortunately, we can't meet the salary you're used to, but I promise I'll try to put together a nice package. When could you start?"

Lucy decided a lower salary was better than none at all. "Is tomorrow too soon?"

"Excellent. I need to pass your application to a couple of board members, but I don't anticipate any problems. I'll call you this afternoon. Would you like a quick tour before you go?"

"I'd love it."

A regal-looking woman in a flowing robe rolled through the door in a wheelchair. She looked near tears. "Can you do my hair?" she asked Alice.

"Your hair?"

"That nitwit girl from the beauty shop is out sick today. I had a nine o'clock appointment for my hair and makeup."

"I'm tied up at the moment, Naomi," Alice said. "Perhaps—"

"Everybody's *tied up*," the woman wailed. "You'd think for what this place costs, I could find one person who had ten minutes to spare." She burst into tears. "I can't let my son see me looking like this."

"I can do your hair," Lucy told the woman. "If it's okay with Alice," she added quickly.

Alice looked surprised. "If you're sure you don't mind."

"I'd be happy to. Perhaps you can fit in a brief tour later."

Alice looked relieved. "Naomi, I want you to meet Lucy Odum. I'm hoping she'll be our new RN."

"Odum?" Naomi frowned. "Did you say Odum? Where have I heard that name?"

"Lucy just moved here from Atlanta," Alice said. She turned to Lucy. "This is Mrs. Naomi Bufford," she added.

Lucy was so stunned at first, she didn't know what to say. The woman had aged considerably over the past fifteen years, but she still carried herself like a queen. Finally, Lucy offered her hand, and Naomi took it, her fingers looking quite frail bearing the weight of several large diamond rings. "Pleased to meet you, Mrs. Bufford," she managed to say, trying to maintain a professional air. "Why don't you point me in the direction of your room, and we can get started."

Still trying to get a grip on her emotions, Lucy rolled Naomi to her quarters and parked the chair before a lavish vanity. The room was decorated in white Queen Anne furniture with powder-blue carpeting and original watercolors done in soft pastels.

She handed Naomi a tissue to dry her eyes. "There now," she said gently. "No need to cry. I'll have you fixed up in a jiffy." She was thankful Naomi hadn't recognized her, as it might have created a great deal of tension between them. Although the woman had never treated her with anything but cool civility when she and Scott had dated, Lucy suspected Scott's father had tainted his wife's opinion of her long ago.

Naomi wiped her eyes. "You don't know what it's like growing old and ugly in a place where nobody cares whether you live or die."

"That's not true, Mrs. Bufford. Of course people care. And you are anything *but* ugly." Lucy reached for a silver-plated brush and began her work. Naomi's hair was long and streaked with gray, but there were still hints of the beautiful auburn color it had once been. She thought about her own mother and how different her life had been compared to Mrs. Bufford's. Although both women had been married to difficult men, Naomi hadn't had to make the same sacrifices her mother had. Of course, she empathized with the woman over losing her son. No parent should have to endure that heartache. At least her other son cared enough to visit her. Lucy looked at the woman's reflection in the mirror. "How would you like me to arrange it?" she asked, trying to sound as normal as possible.

"Just pin it up," Naomi said. "It gets in my way."

"Sometimes a new hairdo can lift your spirits." Lucy braided the woman's hair quickly and fixed it in a fat coil at the nape of her neck. Naomi looked pleased with the results.

"My son will be here any minute," Naomi told her. "He's taking me out for a late breakfast."

Naomi glanced at her diamond wristwatch. "Oh, heavens!" She pushed the wheelchair from the vanity and stood. "Quick, reach into that closet and hand me my salmon-colored linen suit," she said.

Lucy blinked her surprise. "Mrs. Bufford, you're standing!"

"Yes, but my poor old ankles won't hold up for long, so hurry. I'm arthritic, you know."

Lucy reached for the suit and studied the woman closely as she helped her into it. She had seen elderly patients who suffered from crippling arthritis and those who'd become deformed as a result. Naomi looked perfectly fine.

There was a knock at the door. "Just a minute," Lucy called out.

"Oh, there's my son now," Naomi cried. "Hurry and button me up. Just a minute, Scott honey," she called out.

Lucy couldn't mask her confusion. *Scott honey?* Had the poor woman gone daft? She shook herself. No, she'd simply gotten her sons' names mixed up. She wouldn't be the first mother to make such a mistake.

"Okay, come in, sweetie pie," Naomi called out.

The door opened and Scott Bufford walked in, looking more handsome than any man had a right to look. Especially one who was supposed to have died fifteen years earlier.

Lucy opened her mouth to say his name, but the words never made it past her lips. She heard a buzzing sound, and the room spun out of control. Then everything went black.

Scott saw her going down, heard his mother's shriek, and caught the younger woman before she hit the floor. She felt like a rag doll in his arms. He gazed at her, dumbstruck. "What the—?"

"Put her on the bed," Naomi said. "I'll get a wet washcloth."

Scott continued to stare mutely into the woman's face. "Lucy?" he whispered. It couldn't be. He touched her cheek. She certainly *felt* real enough. But what was Lucy Odum doing in Shade Tree, in his mother's bedroom of all places?

Lucy wasn't sure how long she was out, but when she opened her eyes she found herself gazing up into Scott Bufford's bewildered face.

"Oh, my God!" Lucy said, sitting up and pushing herself away from the man she'd thought dead for so long. Naomi was standing directly behind Scott, wringing her hands as though wondering what to make of the whole thing. "What are you doing here?" Lucy asked, the look on her face one of pure terror.

Scott regarded the woman before him. His square jaw tensed visibly, his otherwise full lips thinned in grim lines. "What the hell *is* going on here?" he demanded.

Naomi gasped. "Scott Anthony Bufford, *why* are you talking to my nurse that way?"

"Your *nurse*?" He let his eyes roam Lucy's body. Somehow she'd managed to hold on to those wholesome good looks from high school. "She doesn't look like any nurse *I've* ever seen."

"Oh, Lord." Lucy felt as though she might faint again.

"Do you two know each other?" Naomi asked meekly.

Scott continued to stare at Lucy as though he were seeing a mirage. In a matter of seconds he experienced a gamut of emotions: pain, despair, anger. He fixed her with an accusing look. "I thought we did," he said, "but I was obviously mistaken." He shook himself in an attempt to clear his head. How could this be happening? He turned his attention to his mother, seeing her for the first time. "May we leave now?" he said, deciding he needed some time to get over the shock of seeing Lucy again. He would question her later, when he had his wits about him.

"Yes, sweetie pie, if you're sure you're calm enough to drive. Why, I've never seen you like this. I just have to spray my hair and dab a bit of perfume on my wrists. Oh, where did I put my purse?"

"I'll wait for you in the lobby." He left the room without another word.

Naomi looked near tears as she reached for her perfume bottle and applied the flowery scent on her wrists and behind her ears. "I'm so confused!"

Only then did Lucy realize how badly she was trembling. "It has nothing to do with you, Mrs. Bufford." With shaking hands she reached for the woman's pocketbook and handed it to her.

Lucy pushed Naomi through the door, then asked an aide to take over. She returned to Naomi's room and sat on the bed, thankful for a moment alone. Her features were strained, her normally bright eyes dull with the muddle of disbelief. Scott Bufford alive? No wonder she hadn't found his grave.

But how could that be? She had seen his obituary, dammit!

She continued to sit there, waiting for the trembling to stop, for the lightheadedness to go away. How could something like this have happened? Fifteen years had passed, and all along she'd thought him dead. Her mind reeled; strange and disquieting thoughts nagged her and refused to let go. She'd been duped.

The door opened and Lucy looked up. Alice peeked in. "Are you okay?"

Lucy managed a small, tentative smile as she got up quickly from the bed and started smoothing out the wrinkles. "I'm fine," she said quickly.

"Scott Bufford just paid me a brief visit and demanded I fire you immediately. What's going on, Lucy?"

She colored fiercely. Why would Scott have done such a thing? Her answer was quick in coming. If Aubrey Bufford had managed to convince her Scott was dead, there was no telling what he'd told Scott about her.

"Scott and I used to know each other," she said. "It's a long story, Alice, and it happened years ago."

Alice stood there, hands folded, face clouded with uneasiness. "Well, I don't want to delve into your personal affairs, but Scott Bufford has a lot of clout around here. Not only is he on our board of directors, his family has invested heavily in this facility."

Lucy couldn't think of anything to say. Once again the mighty Buffords had sealed her fate.

Alice hesitated. "I'm in charge of hiring and firing," she said, "but all my decisions have to be approved by the board. I saw no reason why they would reject you. All I can do is talk to Mr. Bufford when he returns. I've always found him to be professional and level-headed. You must have been very close at one time for him to lose his head the way he did."

Lucy nodded. "At one time, yes. But that was fifteen years ago."

Alice nodded, then hesitated before asking her the next question. "You didn't do anything illegal?"

"I've never even had a parking ticket."

"Well, I told Scott you were the best applicant we've had, and I plan to stand by that." She smiled, easing the tension in the room considerably. "If he gives me any more trouble, I'll threaten to send his mother home. She's a handful, that one is."

"I guess it's not easy for her to be confined to a wheelchair," Lucy stated.

"She needs that wheelchair like she needs a hole in her head. She's a hypochondriac and has been for years. It's the only way she knew to get attention from her husband and children, I suppose. After a while, they simply started ignoring her, so she came here, where people *have* to give her undivided attention."

"I'm afraid the muscles in her legs will atrophy if she continues to use the wheelchair," Lucy said, her nursing knowledge nudging aside her more painful personal thoughts.

"Well, if you can think of a way to get her out of it, let me know. Now, how about that tour?"

A tour was the last thing she felt up to doing, but Lucy knew she had to get her emotions under control, and listening to Alice talk would give her a little time to regroup.

They started in the reception area. "As you can see," Alice began, "we try very hard to make Restful Valley look more like a lovely hotel or condominium. Some of our clients—" She paused. "We prefer to call them *clients* instead of *patients*. Anyway, some have been in and out of hospitals for years. By the way, we ask that you don't wear a uniform, just regular clothes if you don't mind. You may wear your nurse's pin, of course, so that everyone is aware of your status."

Lucy nodded, although at the moment she was more concerned whether she would get the job than what she would wear.

She followed Alice into the dining room. Each table

was draped in white and set with what appeared to be expensive china. A basket of fresh flowers sat in the very center. "It looks like an exclusive restaurant," Lucy said.

"Restful Valley is not your run-of-the-mill nursing home," Alice said proudly. "Our clients are well off. They come from all over. It was a real boon to our little town that the investors chose Shade Tree. We're only an hour from the airport, so it's convenient for relatives to visit." She leaned close. "I may as well tell you, there's talk of adding a retirement community for those who aren't in need of assisted care. It would take several years for it to become a reality, of course."

Lucy suspected Scott Bufford had his fingers in that as well, but she didn't say anything. "Think of the job opportunities," she replied instead.

"Exactly."

By the time Lucy had toured the facility and met most of the staff, it was nearly noon. As she said good-bye to Alice and started for the reception room, Scott wheeled Naomi through the double doors. "Can you see your way to your room?" he asked his mother. "I'd like to speak to Miss Odum."

Lucy had no desire to cause another scene. The less they said to each other, the better. Maybe, just maybe, Alice could convince him to hire her despite any problems in the past. She certainly had the credentials; Scott had only to look at her application to see she was perfect for the job. "I'm sort of in a hurry," she said, not quite meeting his gaze as she tried to slide past him. She was much too shaken to talk to him intelligently. Why hadn't her mother told her the truth?

"Oh, I think you can take a few minutes out of your busy schedule to speak with me." He slipped his arm through hers. There was no way to pull free without causing a scene in front of the receptionist, so she went peacefully. Besides, she intended to demand he tell her what had happened to him.

Besides, it was time she found out the truth!

TWO

Lucy let herself be propelled toward a big black Lincoln Continental that smelled of new leather and aftershave. Once Scott joined her in the front seat, they merely stared at each other. Lucy felt a tightness low in her belly. How could she have ever thought him dead, when his entire body pulsed with energy and life?

The years had been good to him, she noted, carving masculine lines into the face of the boy she'd once known. His hair was still as brown as Brazil nuts, still thick and radiant with only a hint of gray at his temples. But it was his eyes that were her undoing, even after all these years. They had been dark and intense when he was seventeen; they were even more so now.

She clasped her hands tightly in her lap. They were moist. They'd been that way when he'd asked her to the school dance in tenth grade, and several months later when he'd given her his bracelet.

In his senior year, he'd given her his class ring and a solid gold chain so she could wear it around her neck. It was the first time she could remember anyone, especially her female classmates, being envious of her. "You have something you want to say to me?" she asked, feeling as vulnerable as she had the first time he'd asked her to unbutton her blouse in the moonlight. She'd been in the eleventh grade, and most of her friends had already had at least one sexual experience. Before long touching her breasts wasn't enough for either of them.

"I tried to have you fired," Scott said, feeling crummy about the whole thing now that his temper had cooled. But what the hell did she expect, he thought, showing up out of the blue and looking every bit as good as he remembered. She had no right to just waltz into town after what she'd put him through.

Lucy noted his rigid jaw. Its squareness had become more defined with age. A small nick near his chin made her wonder if he'd cut himself shaving. She had known him when the only hair that had grown on his face was peach fuzz, long before he'd developed this commanding and polished veneer.

"Yes, I know," she managed to get out, trying to summon enough breath to speak. There were so many things she wanted to tell him, so many questions, although right now she couldn't string enough intelligible words together to make a complete sentence. And she was terribly worried about not having a job.

"I lost my temper. It's just . . . it was a shock seeing you again. After all these years," he added.

His voice was both sensual and masculine, striking a chord deep within her. At the same time, she sensed disapproval. "Yes, well, it was a shock seeing you again too," she said. "I—I thought you were dead."

"No, Lucy," he said. "I'm very much alive. Perhaps if you'd hung around long enough, you would have seen for yourself."

"The doctors said—"

"I don't care what the doctors told you," he said, his words tense and clipped and leaving no room for argument. It irritated him that he should find her so disturbing in every way, even now. He felt his body tighten as he assessed her frankly and counted the ways in which Mother Nature had improved upon her in the aging process. "The doctors were obviously wrong," he added. He paused, trying to get a grip on his emotions. "Look, I don't know what you're doing here, but my mother seems to like you. I promised her I wouldn't make trouble."

"That's awfully kind of you," Lucy said, trying to hide the hurt in her voice when she should have been cheering over her new job. But she *was* hurt. Not to mention confused and feeling very sorry for herself that life had played such a cruel trick on her.

Scott frowned. His dark brows bunched together and two vertical slits appeared directly over his nose, giving him a menacing look. "You and I both know I'm being much kinder than you deserve, seeing as how you deserted me while I lay near death."

"I didn't desert you," she said. "But it's your choice to believe what you wish. What I don't understand is why you didn't look for me once you had recovered."

"Is that what you were hoping I'd do?" he asked. "Actually, I considered it at first. Lucky for me I came to my senses before I made a complete fool of myself." His eyes became as flat and unreadable as a slab of concrete, and Lucy wondered at what point he'd learned to mask his emotions so well. "Why did you walk out on me like that, Lucy? Were you afraid of being stuck with a cripple for the rest of your life?"

She felt as though he'd slapped her. A chill black

silence sprang up between them like an invisible wall. Although Lucy suspected Aubrey Bufford was responsible for Scott's feelings toward her, she was in no condition to try to explain her side of the story. She was still reeling over the fact that he was alive. Perhaps later, when they'd both had a chance to calm down, come to terms with everything, she'd tell him the details.

Right now she needed to be alone.

Lucy reached for the door handle. "I have to go," she said, forcing her voice to remain steady. "You'll talk to Alice Bloom?" she said as though it were a mere afterthought. She was too proud to let him know how much she needed the job.

Scott nodded tersely, relieved the conversation was over. "I'll handle it."

Lucy got out of the car and hurried to her own, her breath coming in shallow, quick gasps that made her wonder if she was on the verge of hyperventilating. She couldn't seem to control the almost spasmodic trembling that overtook her once she pulled from the parking lot. She was so numb that the tears didn't start until she was halfway home.

The phone was ringing when Lucy stepped inside the empty house. She hurried to it and snatched it up.

"This is Alice," the voice said from the other end. "You're hired."

"Oh, good," Lucy said, relief making her dizzy.

"And that's not even the best news," Alice said. "Although it took a little finagling on my part, I was able to match your previous salary."

Lucy closed her eyes. Things were beginning to look up.

That night, as Lucy prepared dinner, she gave her mother the lowdown on her day, including running into Scott Bufford at Restful Valley and fainting in his arms.

Loretta looked up from her sewing and snapped a piece of thread in half with her teeth. "Oh, honey," she said, "I just assumed you knew he was alive. I didn't want to mention his name because I was afraid you'd change your mind about moving back home."

Lucy shook her head. "I thought my heart had stopped beating when he walked through that door and I realized he wasn't dead after all."

Loretta paused and studied her daughter thoughtfully. "Didn't you wonder, *even once*, whether Scott had pulled through the accident?"

Lucy told her about the obituary notice Aubrey had sent her. "You knew he had me transferred to another hospital," she said. "I was in for a couple of weeks, during which time I received both the notice and my payoff."

"Oh, my Lord!" Loretta sputtered and carried on about how she found it hard to believe that even a good-for-nothing snake in the grass like Aubrey Bufford could have done such a thing.

"I never trusted him," Lucy said. "I lived in fear he'd change his mind and come after Kelly, so I moved to Atlanta and tried to get lost in the crowd."

Loretta looked sad. "You don't know how hard it was for me to say good-bye to you and my only grandchild. But I knew you'd be better off on your own than living here with your father." Her eyes misted over and she wiped them. "I kept all the cards you sent. They meant a lot to me." She wrinkled her nose after a moment. "Honey, what are you cooking?"

"Cabbage soup. And don't look at me like that, it happens to be very good."

"Healthy, too, I'll bet," Loretta mumbled, then went back to mending one of Kelly's blouses. "I just don't believe things like this can happen in this day and time. You thinking Scott's dead for fifteen years when he's actually alive. You hiding out from Aubrey so he won't take your baby. Me wondering where you are and if you're okay." She sighed. "You read about such in the newspaper and hear about it on the talk shows, but I always figure someone's just making it up."

Loretta looked sad. "I feel awful for you."

"It's not your fault. You had no way of contacting me. My decision to leave may seem drastic as we look back on it, but at the time I felt it was the only way I could protect Kelly." She paused. "I'd appreciate it if you didn't mention her father to her just now. Naturally, she thinks he's dead. I'll have to break the news to her gently.

"What really bothers me most about this whole situation is the fact that Scott never once tried to look for us. Wasn't he the least bit curious about his daughter?"

Loretta looked sad once more. "Honey, Scott doesn't know about Kelly," she said. "Aubrey told him the baby was born dead. I didn't get wind of it until long after the accident. By then I figured it was too late to say anything one way or the other."

The color drained from Lucy's cheeks. She had to sit down to keep from falling. "How could something like that have happened?" she said in disbelief. "Why didn't you tell him differently?"

Loretta took her hand. "I tried to see Scott a couple of times while he was in the hospital, but Aubrey refused to let him have visitors. As soon as the boy was stable, his daddy moved him out to the house, where he began his physical therapy. Aubrey even hired a security guard to stand at the front entrance. I'm telling you, the place was like a fortress.

"I called and wrote, but Scott never responded, so I figured he wasn't getting my mail or the phone messages." She paused and sighed. "Six months later he married his physical therapist, and before I knew it they had a baby of their own on the way."

Lucy's heart tumbled to her feet. "Scott's married?"

"He was. They moved to Miami for a while so Scott could attend college. When they came back they had a son. His name is James or Jim or Jeff, something like that. Nice-looking boy. Anyway, the marriage lasted only five years before Scott's wife filed for divorce. I would have told him about his daughter then, but I had no way of knowing if you'd have wanted him involved in your new life. For all I knew, you were happily married and didn't want reminders of the past."

Lucy had never felt so confused. Her misery was so acute that she felt physically ill. Scott had known all along she was out there. Not only had he not bothered looking for her, he'd pledged his love to another woman. Obviously what they'd shared before the accident had not meant as much to him as it had to her.

"I don't know why life has to be so complicated," Lucy said, feeling near tears. She *would* have cried had her mother not been there to witness it. Perhaps later, in private, she would cry. She actually looked forward to releasing some of her anguish in her bed pillow.

Loretta put the newly mended blouse down, got up, walked over to her daughter, and hugged her tightly. "I'm sorry, sweetheart. I should have told you all this sooner, but I was afraid you'd change your mind about moving back if you thought you'd have to tangle with that family. I watched Aubrey groom Scott for years so that he could take over the family business when the time came. I can't help but wonder if the boy took on some of his daddy's characteristics as well."

Lucy's hazel eyes flickered with apprehension. She felt a knot of anxiety in her stomach. "You don't think Scott would try to take Kelly from me, do you?"

"He might be mad enough to threaten you with something like that in the beginning," Loretta said, "but it's not likely he'd follow through." She picked up one of Kelly's oxford blouses that was missing a button.

Lucy watched her mother stir through a tin container of buttons for one that would match those on the shirt. "After we eat we're going to take a twenty-minute walk. We're going to walk every evening after dinner and work up to an hour a day."

"Can't say that I'm looking forward to that," Loretta said, rethreading her needle.

Kelly came into the kitchen and joined her mother at the soup pot. "What smells so good?"

"Cabbage soup," Loretta said dourly.

"Did you finish your homework?" Lucy asked.

"Most of it. This school is about six months behind the one in Atlanta. If I'm not careful, I might accidently end up on the honor roll."

"Oh, goodness," Lucy said, dropping a kiss on her daughter's forehead. "We can't have that. What would the neighbors think?"

"Any cute boys?" Loretta asked.

"All she thinks about these days is boys," Lucy muttered. "If only she'd pay that much attention to her studies."

Kelly smiled at her grandmother. "Actually, I have

met a boy I sort of like," she said. "He's younger than me, but I don't care."

"Oh, age doesn't matter," Loretta said. "As long as he's got money in the bank." She ignored the look Lucy shot her. "Is he cute?"

Kelly giggled. "He's like the cutest boy in school." She looked at Lucy. "Mom, I know how you feel about me dating at my age—"

Lucy gasped. "Dating! We agreed you'd wait until you're sixteen."

"Yes, but you know how all my girlfriends in Atlanta got to meet boys at the movies on Friday nights, and you were like the only parent in the free world that didn't allow it? I think it's time you let me do these things. Otherwise, I'll have to sneak around behind your back, and you'll lose all trust in me." The girl had to stop talking long enough to catch her breath.

"Who *is* this boy?" Lucy demanded, knowing she was prying and unable to help herself. How many times had her coworkers accused her of being too strict with Kelly? She knew in her heart why she set such firm limits. She didn't want her daughter to end up pregnant and unmarried the way she had. She didn't want Kelly to end up raising a baby alone.

"I want to know his name and what kind of family he comes from," Lucy said, deciding some habits were harder to break than others.

"I don't know much about his family except that his parents are divorced. His name is Jeff Bufford."

"Oh, my word!" Loretta cried. She gave a gasp, then swallowed hard.

Lucy, in the process of taking a sip of iced tea, felt the glass slip from her fingers and shatter to the floor.

There was silence as Lucy and Loretta exchanged

shocked glances. Kelly looked at her mother speculatively. "Are you guys okay? Mom? Grandma? What's wrong?"

"I swallowed a button," Loretta said. "I stuck it between my teeth so I wouldn't misplace it and—"

"So why are you sucking on your finger?"

"I must've stuck the needle in my finger as well."

Lucy knelt down to pick up the broken pieces of glass. "Let me help you with that," Kelly offered, kneeling beside her. "Why are your hands trembling?"

"Huh? Oh, must be from all the caffeine I drank today. I'm okay. Why don't you finish your homework. Dinner will be ready shortly."

Kelly glanced from her mother to Loretta. "Okay, but everybody sure is acting weird for some reason. Is it because I have a boyfriend?"

"Oh, no," Lucy replied.

"Of course not," Loretta said.

They watched the girl go. "Sorry I broke your glass," Lucy said as she tossed the pieces into the trash. She grabbed a wad of paper towels and started mopping up the spill.

"That glass is the least of your worries," Loretta said. "What are you going to do *now*?"

"I have every intention of telling Kelly the truth," she said. "When I feel the time is right," she added. "The move and changing schools has been a big adjustment for her. I don't want to put too much stress on her."

"Better she find out from you than somebody else."

"Who's going to tell her? Who else knows but us? Don't forget, Aubrey Bufford convinced everybody the baby died. I don't know how he managed to keep the hospital staff from talking, but if he can send me an obituary notice on his son, he can do just about anything."

"You know there's a print shop in his plant here," Loretta said.

Lucy froze. "No, I didn't."

"Well, you *must* know the Shade Tree plant isn't the only orange juice processing facility the Buffords own. He has several, in fact. Aubrey used to run a monthly newsletter for his employees. We called it his brag sheet because that's all it was really. He made sure everybody knew his plants were superior to his competitors' and told us what a difference he was making in the community. I'm sure he could print anything he wanted in that shop, including a fake obituary."

Lucy pressed her lips together grimly. Oh, how Aubrey must've hated her, to go to such lengths. "That's sick," she said.

"I suppose he was willing to go to any extreme to see that his oldest son didn't marry into the wrong family. Poor Scott ended up with somebody he didn't love."

"Well, that's in the past now," Lucy said wearily. "I suppose all we can do is to get on with our lives." In her heart, though, she knew it wouldn't be easy letting go of the past when every time she looked at her daughter she would think of Scott. And what about when Scott found out about Kelly? She suspected, no matter what his feelings toward her, he would want to be a part of his daughter's life. His presence would be a constant reminder of the love they'd shared and lost.

"I'm sorry," Loretta said, touching her arm lightly. "I shouldn't have just blurted it out the way I did. I had no idea you'd feel this strongly about Scott after all these years."

"I'm okay," Lucy said. "It was just a shock hearing

he'd married and all. Not that he didn't have every right, of course," she added quickly. "Especially if he'd thought I'd just abandoned him." Once again she wondered what Aubrey Bufford had told his son.

Lucy didn't have much of an appetite at dinner. She tried to pay attention to what Kelly was saying about one of her classes, but her sense of concentration was sorely lacking. The day had taken its toll on her, and she longed for a hot bath and a few minutes of privacy.

Once they'd finished the meal, Kelly cleaned the table while the women washed and dried the dishes. Kelly had just disappeared into the bedroom, when the doorbell rang. "Are you expecting company?" Lucy asked her mother.

Loretta, up to her elbows in sudsy water, shook her head. "Would you mind answering it?"

Lucy hurried into the living room and opened the door. The smile on her face died when she found Scott standing on the other side of the threshold.

"We need to talk," he said, his tone as cool as the night air.

"Now?" Lucy glanced over her shoulder to make sure Kelly hadn't come out of the bedroom.

"Now."

Her curiosity piqued, Lucy grabbed her coat from the nearby wall rack and stepped out onto the front porch, where Scott waited, handsome as ever in the soft glow of the porch light. His expression offered no clues as to why he was there. Did he know about Kelly? It suddenly occurred to her that Scott's son might have mentioned the new girl at school and raised his father's suspicions. No, that wasn't it. Aubrey would have convinced Scott the baby hadn't survived. So, why was he here?

"Do you mind if we chat on the porch?" Lucy asked, closing the door behind her before he had a chance to respond one way or another.

"That's fine," he said curtly. "This won't take long." He took a step closer and studied her in the dim light. He noted the subtle changes. Her features were sharper, more defined, but she was still as pretty as she'd been in high school. He could still remember what her skin felt like. He supposed it had something to do with the fact she'd been his first love, and that she'd carried his baby; otherwise, he would have felt nothing for her. As he stood there, trying to gather his thoughts, he deliberately shut out any awareness of her.

Lucy tried to hide her hurt feelings from his probing stare. She could have been a complete stranger for all the warmth he showed. "Why'd you come back, Lucy?" he asked, deciding it was best to get everything out in the open.

She remembered a time when they'd been so close, it was hard to tell where one left off and the other began. She remembered their first stolen kiss behind the gym at school, the dances and parties they'd attended. She remembered the first time they'd made love. But none of that seemed to matter to Scott. His coolness and indifference toward her tore at her already aching heart. It was as if he'd been brainwashed, as if all the meaningful times they'd shared had been surgically removed from his mind.

"You heard my father died," she said, giving no clue as to her thoughts. "I'd planned to come only for his funeral, but when I saw how poorly my mother was doing—"

"What's wrong with Loretta?" he asked sharply.

Lucy hoped she hadn't spoken out of turn. After all,

Scott was her mother's employer. "She has diabetes, and from what I've seen, she's not taking proper care of herself. I thought I could help." She wasn't about to tell him guilt had motivated her. No matter how much she'd hated her father, how frightened she'd been of Aubrey, she shouldn't have cut off communication with her mother. In a way, she supposed she had been punishing the woman for not having left Darnel.

"How long will you be staying?" he asked.

Lucy paused. "I don't know. Six months, six years, why, does it matter?"

"It matters." He glanced away from her, but not before she caught a glimpse of the sorrow in his eyes. "How can you even show your face in this town after what you did?" he asked.

She studied his tense jaw, determined to find the answers she'd been seeking. "What exactly *did* I do, Scott?"

"You walked out on me when it looked like I was dying."

"You *assumed* I walked out. What makes you think I wasn't *ordered* to leave?"

"I knew you'd try to dump all the fault on my father."

"And I knew you'd take up for him. You were always blind to the terrible things he did." Lucy could feel the tears stinging her eyes. "You don't know what it was like, Scott. You were *dying*. *Dying!* The doctor that performed brain surgery on you said you'd never come out of that coma.

"I don't think you can appreciate what a miracle it is for you to be alive today . . . and functioning as a normal human being." She paused and the tears fell. "It was awful, Scott. I couldn't stand to watch you die like that. Your father didn't want me there, and your poor mother was so ill, she couldn't leave her own bed. It was a nightmare." She didn't bother to tell him that her own father had called the hospital drunk and told her not to come home with her illegitimate brat.

Scott noted the tears and looked away. There was a time her tears would have brought him to his knees emotionally, but he'd been a mere boy and hadn't understood that some females used them to their advantage. Hell, she could probably summon them at will. "That still doesn't explain why you took my father's money and left town."

Lucy gazed back at him. He'd obviously been angry for a long time, and it wasn't likely he'd get over it anytime soon. She wasn't sure he was ready to learn about Kelly. "I had every right to that money, Scott," she said, holding her head high.

"Why?"

"Because, I—" She couldn't find the words. He was so angry now. If she told him about his daughter, he'd probably lose his temper completely. "It was my only hope of getting away. And of making something of myself," she said at last.

"You've always been a taker, Lucy. Even back when we were planning to get married, I knew I loved you more than you could ever love me."

"That's not true. I gave as much as I received."

"I pined away for you for months," he said. "I kept wishing I'd died and never woke up from that coma."

"You didn't pine away too long," she said stiffly. "From what I understand, you married within six months of my leaving. I hear you have a son."

The frown deepened into a menacing scowl. He had never looked more dangerous. "Keep my ex-wife out of this, Lucy. She was there to pick up the pieces when you turned your back on me. As for my son—" He paused. "He's been the only bright spot in my life."

"Why did you come here, Scott? If you dislike me so much, why bother coming by at all?"

"I just want to get a few things straight with you. I don't want you interfering in my life now that you're back."

She was amazed that he still had the power to hurt her. "You came *here*," she reminded him smugly, then added with a smirk, "maybe you don't hate me as much as you think you do."

He glared at her. She had always been able to read him like the back of a cereal box. She had known from the beginning what she did to him physically *and* emotionally, and she'd used it to her advantage. His gaze slid downward, then locked with hers once more. "What kind of game are you playing, Lucy?" He stepped closer, so close, he could smell the gardenia-scented shampoo she used in her hair. "Did you come back to see if I still had the hots for you? Or did you just run out of money?"

"Go to hell."

"I've already been there and back over you, baby."

Lucy took a step back and found herself flattened against the screen door. The feral look in his eyes startled her. This was not the boy she had known and loved. He'd become a man, raw and powerful and presently filled with loathing for her. She was afraid. Afraid that he might make Aubrey Bufford look tame once he finished with her. Still, she held her head high and refused to give in to the fear.

"Please leave," she said, her voice trembling now.

"Not until I get some answers," he replied curtly. He edged closer, boldly pressing his body against hers, then curling a hand around her neck and flicking his thumb across the base of her throat. Her pulse skittered wildly.

Lucy shivered and turned away from him. She would not allow him to see the pain and embarrassment he was causing her.

Scott noted her flushed cheeks with a sense of pride, saw the hardened nipples beneath her blouse where her jacket fell open. He longed to fasten his lips around them. Fifteen years had passed, and she was still as responsive to his touch as she'd been the first time. It did his heart good to know he could still arouse her. With his index finger he turned her face so that she had no choice but to look at him. He lowered his head, his lips brushed hers.

"Scott—" His name was a whimper on her lips. "Please," she whispered.

"Please what?" This time when he touched her lips, the kiss was almost brutal. His tongue thrust deeply into her mouth, exploring and plundering, leaving no part untouched. His grip on her was both sweet and painful. Lucy had no choice but to give in to his demanding touch. He broke the kiss and nipped her bottom lip with his teeth.

He wants to hurt me, she thought. Punish me for hurting him. The thought saddened her. She realized she was crying.

Scott saw the fresh tears and hated himself for being the cause. He'd meant to cause her pain, and he'd succeeded. So why did he feel like kicking himself?

A sudden noise jolted them apart. The door opened and Lucy turned. Kelly peered through the screen. "Mom, are you out here?"

Lucy sniffed and wiped the tears from her cheeks.

She tried to smile as she turned toward her daughter. "Go back in the house, Kelly," she said. "I'll be right in."

"Is something wrong?" The girl sounded anxious. "Why are you crying? Who is that man?"

Lucy stood there for a moment wondering what to say or do next. She sensed the timing wasn't right. Scott was much too angry to meet his daughter for the first time. "This is just an old friend of mine, sweetheart. We just . . . he just told me some sad news is all. Now close the door, I'll be right in."

Kelly did as she was told. Lucy turned her attention back to Scott and found him studying his shoes. He almost looked embarrassed. "I take it that's your daughter?"

"Yes."

"From her age, I'd say you didn't waste any time finding my replacement." The look in his eye told her he was thinking the worst. Not only had she gotten pregnant by him out of wedlock, she had not bothered to marry Kelly's father either. She was tempted to let him keep on believing it, then realized she owed it to her daughter to tell him the truth.

"Don't you want to know how old she is?" Lucy asked.

He shrugged. "Should I?"

"She's fifteen, Scott." Lucy looked directly into his eyes as she said it. "Want to know when she was born? July 3, 1980, the day of the car accident." She had the satisfaction of seeing his look of indifference turn to incredulity. "You're so smart, *you* figure it out. When you do, give me a call." She let herself into the house and slammed the door.

THREE

You're so smart, you figure it out. What the hell was *that* supposed to mean?

Muttering a mouthful of expletives, Scott strode to his car and climbed in, then sat and gazed at the house as though half expecting Lucy to come out and explain herself. What was she trying to pull *now*? Was she trying to pass the girl off as his daughter? Was the woman totally without scruples?

The baby didn't make it, Scott. It was stillborn.

He plunged his fingers into his hair and shook his head, trying to make sense of a world that had suddenly gone haywire. If he weren't so angry, he would march right back to the door and demand an explanation. As it was, he didn't want to give Lucy the satisfaction of knowing she'd given him such a jolt. He started his engine and backed out of the driveway, glancing at the house through his rearview mirror and wondering if Lucy had lost her marbles.

Scott drove around for the next half hour, thinking over their conversation. How could she possibly hope to make him believe the child was his? Was it money that motivated her? He drove some more and ended up at a friend's house.

Jim Burke was the administrator for Shade Tree General Hospital and a good friend to boot. He wasn't originally from that area, he came from Texas, but everybody treated him as though he'd been born and raised in Shade Tree. He was a widower with two grown children. He opened the door the minute Scott knocked.

"Scott, what brings you here?" he asked. "Not that you need an excuse," he added, looking happy to see him. He was dressed in dark slacks, a white shirt, and a loose cardigan. He carried a Dickens novel in one hand.

"Am I interrupting anything?" Scott asked, although he knew better. Jim was only ten or twelve years older than he was, but the man spent most of his time with his nose tucked between the pages of a book.

"Of course not. Come into my study, and I'll pour us a brandy. Frankly, you look like you could use one. What's up, buddy?"

Scott waited until he'd poured the drinks and they were seated. "I need a favor, Jim," he said, his voice sounding desperate even in his own ears.

"Sounds serious."

"It concerns a girl by the name of Lucy Odum. She supposedly gave birth to a stillborn baby in 1980. July third to be exact. I'd like the details."

The man arched one brow. "You know that's confidential."

"I wouldn't have come to you if it wasn't important."

Jim looked thoughtful. After a moment, he reached for the telephone and dialed. "Give me Medical Records, please." He smiled at Scott as he waited. "We keep only one girl on at night, so this might take a while." He took a sip of his drink. "Hello? This is Jim Burke, is this Sissy? Hi, Sissy, how come you're working the night shift?"

Scott squirmed in his chair as the two chatted, then took a drink of his brandy and tried not to look impatient.

"Do me a sweet favor, Sissy," Jim drawled, winking at Scott as if to let him know he could pour on the charm when the occasion presented itself. "I want you to go back into the old files and see if we have something on a Lucy Odum." He looked at Scott. "Is that O-d-u-m?"

"Yeah."

"That's right, Sissy. We're talking July 3, 1980, and this woman supposedly gave birth to a stillborn. I'd like the facts if you can find them. Yes, I'm at home." He hung up. "She'll get back to us as soon as she can." He took a sip of his brandy and eyed Scott over the rim of his glass. "What's going on, pal?"

Scott wondered how much he should tell, then reminded himself Jim was one of his closest friends and would never repeat what was told him in confidence. "You remember I once told you I was in a serious car accident just after I graduated high school?"

"Yes. There was a fatality, I believe."

Scott nodded. "The driver that hit my car was intoxicated. He died at the scene. Anyway, my girlfriend and I were on our way to the hospital, she was in labor, you see."

"Lucy Odum?"

"Right. Fortunately, she escaped with only a few broken bones. I was in a coma for a month and not expected to live."

"And the baby was born dead?"

"So I was told. Now, fifteen years later, Lucy's back, and she's got a daughter she claims belongs to me."

"Who told you the baby was stillborn?"

"My father."

"Would he lie about something like that?"

Scott pondered it. "I wish I knew the answer to that. He was so much against me marrying Lucy that I think he would have done anything to stop it. What I don't understand is how he would have gotten the staff at the hospital to go along with it."

"What makes you think they did?"

"Nobody told me any different. Wouldn't somebody have said something?" He looked thoughtful. "Damn."

"What?"

"I wasn't out of that coma but a few days when my father insisted I be moved home. You know how large our dining room is? He turned it into an infirmary and hand-picked the staff, including my physical therapist."

"Whom you later married," Jim said.

"Right." Scott looked thoughtful. "I thought he moved me so I'd be more comfortable. It never occurred to me he was trying to keep something from me."

"With any luck, you'll know by the time you leave here this evening," Jim said gently.

The men sipped their drinks in silence, eyeing the phone.

It rang, and they both jumped. Jim snatched it up and spoke. "Good grief, Sissy, you're faster than a speeding locomotive." He reached for a sheet of paper and scribbled on it for several minutes, while Scott tried to remain calm. "You're a doll, Sissy." Jim hung up.

Scott leaned forward, clasping his hands together between his knees. "Did you find out anything?"

"I'm not sure you want to hear this."

"Tell me anyway."

"Okay, our records show that seventeen-year-old

Lucy Anne Odum gave birth to a baby girl on July 3rd, 1980, at 10:37 P.M. Although the mother had suffered a number of contusions and lacerations, not to mention a broken wrist, arm, and clavicle in a car accident, the baby was born without injury, weighing in at eight pounds five ounces. As soon as mother and baby were stabilized, they were moved by ambulance to another hospital two hours away."

Scott was jolted to the soles of his feet by the news. "My God, she wasn't lying. I have a daughter."

"Is this good news, Scott?"

He shook his head. "I don't know. Right now I'm too dazed to think."

"Tell me something," Jim said. "The girl is what, fifteen years old? Why is Lucy just now getting around to telling you about her?"

"She claims she thought I was dead." He sighed heavily. "Supposedly, that's what my father told her."

"And she never came back to see for herself?"

Scott shook his head. "My father paid her to stay away, and that's what she did."

"So why is she back now?"

"It's a long story, and I've taken up enough of your time." Scott drained the rest of his brandy and stood. "Thanks, Jim, for the information. I've got to do some heavy thinking."

The other man walked Scott to the front door. "How's that handsome son of yours?"

"Fine. His mother tells me he's got a girlfriend. An older woman, of all things."

"Speaking of your ex-wife, how is she? I run into her at the hospital now and then, but we don't get a chance to chat much."

"Okay. I keep hoping she'll meet someone, but she

claims she's too busy with her job." Even as he spoke of Amy he couldn't help but feel a twinge of guilt. She'd been a good wife and mother, but he hadn't loved her. He hadn't thought it mattered when he married her, after all, they were great friends if not lovers. It must have mattered to Amy, because she divorced him three years later.

Scott said good night and walked to his car. The temperature must have dropped while he was inside, because he suddenly felt cold. He huddled deeper into his jacket as he made his way to his car. He drove around for an hour, wondering what to do now that he knew he had a daughter.

Lucy started her new job the following day. She felt a bit nervous; Restful Valley had close to one hundred patients, and she was the only registered nurse. Of course, there were a couple of LPNs and a half-dozen nurse's aides, but Lucy still suffered from first-day jitters as she stepped into her small office.

She spent the morning getting acquainted with some of the patients and the staff, which included one doctor whom she suspected was a bit on the egotistical side. He dressed as though he were on his way to lunch at an exclusive country club.

Scott was waiting for her when she stepped outside carrying a small brown sack containing her lunch. She spotted him sitting on a bench near the front door and came to an abrupt halt. "What are you doing here?" she said, none too happy to see him after the way he'd acted the previous night.

"That should be obvious. I'm sitting in the cold waiting for you to go to lunch."

"This is Florida. It doesn't get that cold." Actually, the day had turned out quite pleasant, which is why she'd decided to eat her lunch outside in the fresh air. She told him as much.

"Mind if I join you?" he asked.

"Would it matter if I did?"

"Could we stop fighting long enough to talk?" he said.

"We're not fighting. But if you become rude, then I'll have no choice but to discontinue this conversation."

He almost smiled. She'd always had spunk. That was one of the things that had attracted him in the beginning. While a number of girls had been more than happy to be seen with him, Lucy Odum had acted as though she were doing him a favor by going out with him. He suspected her attitude had something to do with being Darnel Odum's daughter and the need to prove herself. "Okay, fair enough," he said.

Lucy walked toward a group of picnic tables, and Scott followed, noting how professional she looked in a deep red wool jacket and matching skirt. Her blouse was as crisp as a new dollar bill, her hair sleeked back and fastened in a gold barrette. She wore little makeup and there was a radiance about her that never could have been accomplished by artificial means. She was polished and exuded self-confidence. One would never have guessed she was the product of a simple mill worker and a crude drunk.

Lucy selected a table and sat down, taking care not to snag her pantyhose as she did so. Scott remained standing, obviously waiting for her to invite him to sit. She would have had to be blind not to notice how good he looked in his charcoal suit and multicolored tie. Nevertheless, she sensed a restlessness about him. He was coiled tight and ready for action. He was on a mission, and she knew he wouldn't leave until he accomplished what he'd come for.

"Okay, you may join me," she said.

Scott sat opposite her and waited until she'd pulled a sandwich and diet soft drink from her sack. "What'd you pack?" he said.

"Tuna fish sandwich. You're welcome to half, but you probably don't eat tuna fish."

He looked offended. "I've eaten it plenty of times," he said, although in all honesty he couldn't remember when. He wondered why it mattered one way or the other.

She took a bite of her sandwich and waited. "Well? You must have a reason for being here."

He shifted on the bench. "I did some checking last night and learned you did in fact give birth to a baby girl the day of our accident."

"I'll bet Aubrey taught you that."

He shot her a blank look. "Taught me what?"

"To check out everybody's story ahead of time."

His jaw tensed. "If you're suggesting my father was cautious in his business dealings, you're correct. He didn't get where he was by letting people cheat him."

"If people tried to cheat him, it was because of the way he treated them. I know how he worked his employees, I saw the toll it took on my mother." She leaned closer. "I also saw his migrant camps. They weren't fit for dogs. Don't try to convince me he was a good man."

A muscle ticked in Scott's jaw. The migrant camps had been a bone of contention between his father and him for years. Scott had won that battle by threatening to leave the family business. The camps were now kept clean and free from mice and roaches and the facilities in good working order.

But none of this was Lucy's business. "I didn't come here to discuss my father's shortcomings," he said at last. "I'm here about our daughter."

"Her name is Kelly," Lucy said.

"And you waited fifteen years to tell me."

"We've already discussed my reasons."

He clasped his hands together on the table. "So now that I know, what do you expect from me?"

Lucy gazed at his hands and noted they'd broadened and become more masculine. She remembered how proud she'd been to hold them when they'd dated. It was no secret Scott could have had any girl he wanted back then. The fact that he'd chosen her, Darnel Odum's daughter, had undoubtedly surprised their classmates as much as her. But what had touched her deeply was that he had approached her nervously, almost humbly when he'd asked for that first date. She had expected Aubrey Bufford's son to be on the arrogant side.

He'd been young and naive at the time. Aubrey hadn't yet left his mark. She looked up. His brown eyes were guarded. "This is about money, isn't it?"

He shrugged. "Isn't it always?"

"You've grown bitter."

"With good reason, I might add."

Lucy closed her eyes and counted to ten. She was not going to lose her temper. She took a deep breath, opened her eyes, and regarded him coolly. "No, Scott, this isn't about money. I took what your father offered because I was desperate to escape this town and determined to build a life for Kelly and me. I don't need anything from you now as far as material things."

"So why'd you even bother to tell me she was mine?" he said.

Lucy glanced down at her uneaten sandwich. "Because I owe it to Kelly to tell her who her father is, and when I do, she's probably going to want to meet you. I don't want you to say or do anything that might hurt her."

"I'm not some ogre, Lucy," he said, wondering how she had managed to make him feel like the bad guy all of a sudden.

"Frankly, I don't know *who* you are anymore."

"That makes us even, then, because I don't know you either."

She was thoughtful. "Okay, as your daughter's mother, I suppose you have a right to know what I'm about. Ask me anything."

"Really?"

She nodded.

"Okay, I wake up from a month-long coma and learn the love of my life has left town without so much as a fare-thee-well. What was I supposed to do?"

She took a deep breath. "First thing you do is concentrate on getting better. Next, you hire a private investigator, which you could have easily afforded. Then, once you find that person, you ask for their side of the story."

He stared back at her. "I don't believe this. You're trying to dump the blame in my lap now."

She shook her head sadly. "There is no *blame* here, Scott," she said, although in all honesty she knew she would blame Aubrey Bufford for the rest of her life. "It happened, okay? We can't go back and change the past. All we can do is look toward the future."

"Are you actually suggesting you and I have a future?" he asked.

His words hurt, and it amazed her that he had that power after all these years. "Where Kelly is concerned, yes. You owe it to Kelly and yourself to try and get to know each other. We owe it to Kelly to at least remain civil."

"I have another question," he said.

She checked her wristwatch. "Okay."

"Didn't you ever wonder, even once, if I'd somehow pulled through?"

She sighed. He was determined to lash out at her, and perhaps it was a healthy way for him to release all those pent-up emotions. She could bring up the obituary notice, of course, but she saw no reason to hurt Scott further by revealing the monstrous act his father had committed. Besides, he probably wouldn't believe her. As far as she could see, he'd filled his father's shoes quite nicely: so well, in fact, that she wondered if he would be a good influence on Kelly. Nevertheless, she had to give him a chance.

"Your prognosis was not good," she said. "I was told you wouldn't hold out another twenty-four or forty-eight hours, and your father made it plain I was not welcome at your deathbed. As for my reasons for leaving Shade Tree, I had plenty." She paused. "But none of it really matters anymore, does it? I know I'm fifteen years late, but I'm offering you the chance to get to know your daughter. The decision is yours, Scott."

He seemed to ponder it. "How do I know you won't run off again? How do I know I won't become attached to the girl, only to have you pack your bags in the middle of the night and leave?"

"You're going to have to trust me."

He looked away because he didn't want her to know the old wounds still hurt him when his defenses were down. Everything had happened so fast; first her arrival, then her announcement that he had a daughter. He'd thought he was ready, but he needed time to absorb it all. The next time he faced Lucy, he would be better equipped emotionally.

"I trusted you once, Lucy," he said, "and look what it got me." He climbed from the bench. "I don't blame Kelly for that, of course, and I have every intention of getting to know her, with or without your permission." He started to walk away.

"When will you let me know?" Lucy asked.

He glanced over his shoulder. "It's been fifteen years. Surely another day or two won't make any difference."

She could see that he was overwhelmed, but what man wouldn't be after all she had revealed in just a matter of days? This was not the time to tell him that his son and their daughter were on the verge of a relationship; but she knew she couldn't put off telling him much longer. She would give him a few days to adjust, *then* tell him.

It was Saturday. Scott was sitting in his office at the plant trying to make sense of a production report he'd been handed. He didn't usually work on weekends, but he'd felt restless. Jeff had spent the night with a friend and wouldn't arrive home until later. He was eager to see the boy. They'd spent the past week together since Amy was away at a convention, but Jeff would return home with his mother the following day.

He and Amy shared joint custody of the boy even though Scott was more than fair when it came to financial obligations. He'd paid cash for a newly built Cape Cod in an upper-class neighborhood so that his ex-wife and son could live in a nice house. He'd felt it was the least he could do after he'd failed her so.

He had been stunned when, after five years of marriage, Amy had asked for a divorce. The question that had come into his mind was *why?* He was a good husband and father as far as he could see, but Amy claimed it wasn't enough. She wanted the love and passion, the secret smiles lovers shared. He tried for a while, but she saw that his heart wasn't in it.

"You don't love me, Scott," she'd said. "You never have. You're still stuck on Lucy. I say we end it while we can still be friends."

Luckily that friendship was still intact. They had disagreements now and then, mostly over Jeff, but they were usually resolved quickly. Scott knew the reason for their amicable relationship. When you weren't emotionally involved with a woman, there was little she could say or do to hurt you.

That's why Lucy frightened him, scared the everliving daylights out of him. She was still under his skin, he desired her now more than he had at seventeen. There was one major difference in his feelings toward her, however. He didn't trust her.

Scott glanced up when someone knocked at his door. "It's open," he called out. He was jolted when a second later Lucy Odum stuck her head through. It was eerie, as though by thinking of her he'd managed to conjure her up in the flesh. Then he reminded himself he'd thought of little else since her return. He stood and rubbed his palms down the front of his jeans. Only then did he realize they were damp. "Yes?"

"Am I disturbing you?"

What a question to ask, he thought. But then, she had no idea how he'd lain awake the night before thinking about her, *fantasizing* about her in that red skirt, shoved up to her waist, riding him hard. It bewildered him that he could harbor so many conflicting emotions toward her while at the same time he wanted her in his bed.

"I had to drop off my mother's medicine," she said. "Could I speak with you a moment?" The medicine wasn't the only reason she was there; she had to tell him about Jeff and Kelly.

"Come in."

She approached his desk slowly. "This won't take long."

He watched her cross the room. She was wearing snug jeans and a white sweater. She was not a petite woman—she was five seven or eight—nor was she reed-thin like the models who preened at him from magazine covers at the checkout stand at the supermarket. She looked fresh, not to mention soft and curvy and very feminine. He had visions of caressing that honey-colored skin, of sinking into her so deeply, she'd gasp, maybe even cry out. What was it about her that made him want to make love to her one moment and hurt her the next? Was he losing his mind?

Lucy saw the play of emotions on his face and wondered at them. "Scott? Are you okay?"

"What do you want?" he asked tersely.

She arched one brow. The man was in a sour mood and probably had no desire to hear what she had to tell him. She motioned to the chair in front of his desk. "May I sit down?" He nodded and reclaimed his seat as well.

"I'll come right to the point," she said. "Are you aware that your son has a girlfriend?"

He blinked several times, wondering what that could

possibly have to do with her. "Jeff mentioned he liked someone, but I didn't ask for details. I figured he'd tell me when he was ready. Why are you concerned about my son?"

"His girlfriend is Kelly. Our daughter."

"Oh." He raked a finger through his hair. Finally, he shrugged. "They're fourteen and fifteen years old, for heaven's sake. What does it matter at this point?"

"I don't think it's a good idea for them to think of themselves as girlfriend and boyfriend. Also, they'll be embarrassed about it when they learn the truth. Kids might tease them."

"Just how involved *are* they?"

"I think he walks her to class. They talk on the phone a lot."

"So you're suggesting we nip it in the bud before it's too late."

"Exactly. And I think we should tell them the truth together. There's a coffee shop in town. We could meet later today and get everything out in the open. Unless you're not ready."

He was a little nervous about meeting Kelly for the first time, but it was only fair she know the truth. It was up to her if she wanted a relationship with him, although he hoped she would.

"Have you thought about what we should say?" he asked.

"I think honesty is our best policy."

He suddenly looked amused. "It's a bit late for that, isn't it, Luce? I mean, the girl's fifteen years old. I would've thought you'd have mentioned me before now, even if you truly thought me dead."

"I *did* mention you. I told her you were dead! If I

failed to elaborate, I had my reasons. They seemed right at the time."

He stood and placed his hands flat on the desk. "Did you ever wonder whether they were right for Kelly?"

"Of course I did. It's not as if I left her completely in the dark."

"What exactly *did* you tell her?"

Lucy picked at her sweater. "That we were married for a short time—"

"More lies."

"I didn't want her to know she was born out of wedlock. Is that so wrong?"

"How did you explain the fact that both of you use your maiden name?"

"I just told her I took my name back after your death because it was less painful for me."

His face was unreadable. "Go on."

"I told her you'd died in a car accident, which was the truth as I knew it. I framed your senior high school picture and put it on her night table so she'd know what you looked like."

"How thoughtful." He rounded the desk and sat on the edge in front of her. "Wasn't she curious to know more? Didn't she wonder who her grandparents were, whether there were aunts and uncles on either side of the family?"

"Of course. I told her I wasn't close to your family and that I wanted absolutely nothing to do with my father." She paused. "You have to understand, Scott. By the time Kelly was old enough to ask me these questions, we'd built a good life for ourselves. It's not as if we didn't have plenty of friends in Atlanta."

"And in all that time you never married or took a lover," he said.

Her mouth dropped open in surprise. "What kind of question is that?"

"I'm entitled to know what sort of lifestyle my daughter was exposed to. Was it healthy and nurturing, or did you drag in one paramour after another?"

Lucy stood. "This conversation is finished," she said. "I should have known we couldn't talk."

He stood as well and rounded the desk. They were so close, Lucy could feel the heat bouncing off his chest, could smell his aftershave, see the pores in his handsome face. But she refused to back off and give him the upper hand. She wondered if he knew he already had it.

"This conversation isn't finished until I say it is," he said. "After all, you started it."

Lucy tried to compose herself. She felt the leather chair at the back of her knee; it prevented her from taking a step back. Her voice trembled when she spoke. "I came here to discuss our daughter, but you insist on turning it into a boxing match. . . ."

He held his hands out as though perfectly innocent. "All I did was inquire as to our daughter's upbringing. Isn't that a fair question for a father to ask?"

"You know me better than that, Scott."

"Not anymore, babe. We're practically stangers."

"You don't believe that. As for whether or not our daughter was raised in a fit environment, the answer is yes. But I don't think that's what you're truly looking for here. What you really want to know is whether I've slept with another man during the past fifteen years, and *that* is none of your damn business." She turned to go.

He closed his hand around her upper arm. "Stop."

She yanked free and faced him once more. "What do you mean, *stop*? I don't take orders from you."

He plunged his fingers into his hair. He saw the anger in her face and knew he deserved it. Where did he get off asking about her sex life and ordering her around as though he had the right. Get a grip, he told himself.

He sighed. "Damn, Lucy, I lose it every time we're together."

She inched her head high. "So I've noticed. I can't open my mouth without you jumping down my throat. If we're going to continue like this, then I don't see how we can possibly work together where Kelly's concerned."

He went back around the desk and sank into his chair, giving her a dejected look. "I feel like the whole world has turned upside down. I thought my anger toward you had finally been put to rest, but then, one look at you, and it all came rushing back." He eyed her. "It's always been there, Luce, lying just below the surface."

She felt her eyes grow moist. "I'm sorry you feel you have to hate me, Scott. I was forced to make a decision no seventeen-year-old girl should have to make. I made my decision based on what facts I had. As I've said before, we can't go back and change the past. All we can do is look to the future. It's not too late to be a father to Kelly, but I can't see that happening unless you learn to control some of this rage toward me. I'm not about to place Kelly in the middle of a dysfunctional relationship. If you wish to see her, then I insist you treat me with some degree of respect."

"I don't have to do a damn thing," he said belligerently "She's my daughter, and I have every *right* to see her. Don't think for one minute I won't drag you into court to prove it."

She noted the venom in his eyes and wished she'd never told him about the child they'd brought into the world. He was as vindictive as his father had been. "Your name's not on the birth certificate, Scott," she said. "You can't prove anything."

He snapped his head back as though he'd been punched in the face, then bolted from his chair. "What?" He shook his head as if to clear it. "What do you mean, it's not on there? Who did you list as the father?"

"I didn't. I was afraid your father might have a change of heart and try to take Kelly from me. For that very reason, I decided not to give out any more information than I absolutely had to."

He pressed one hand against his forehead as though it ached. "This just keeps getting crazier by the minute," he said. Finally, he crossed his arms over his broad chest and regarded her. "I could have a judge order a blood test, you know."

She shrugged. "And I'll fight you every step of the way. After all, I'm not asking you for child support. I'm more than capable of providing for Kelly."

He glowered at her. "You have no clue what it'd cost to battle this out in a courtroom, do you, Lucy? Correct me if I'm wrong, but I don't believe you can afford to hire a team of lawyers to fight me."

"You'd risk turning this whole thing into a three-ring circus?" she said coolly. She crossed her arms in front of her. "Go ahead, Scott. I'll do what I have to to protect Kelly, just as I did before."

He sighed heavily, tiredly. "Okay, you win this round, Luce," he said. "I promise to behave like a perfect gentleman when our daughter is present. Not because I think you deserve it, but because I'm determined to make this a pleasant experience for Kelly."

She knew it had cost him to admit defeat. "Thank you."

"Don't thank me. You and I aren't finished yet."

She shrugged. "Very well."

As he gazed back at her he had to give her credit; she had backbone. She'd left town because she'd been afraid of his father, but he seriously doubted the old man would have been able to intimidate her today. There was a steely-eyed confidence about her that told him she could give as well as she could take.

"Okay, we'll meet," he said at last. "But I don't want to tell Kelly and Jeff the truth in a public place. It might get emotional." He was thoughtful, carefully weighing the suggestion he was about to make. "Why don't the two of you come over for burgers tonight at my place. We can break the news then. In private." Secretly he knew he wanted to be on his own turf, where he'd feel less vulnerable. Just in case the kids didn't take the news well.

Although Lucy suspected she'd feel uncomfortable in his house, she didn't want to do battle with him on every little issue. "What time should Kelly and I plan to arrive?"

"Why don't you come around four? She and Jeff can swim before dinner."

"It's a little cold for that, isn't it?"

"I have an enclosed pool that I spend a fortune heating. After my father's heart attack, I realized I'd better get in shape."

She found her gaze straying from his face to his broad chest and shoulders and couldn't help but note he was in perfect physical condition. Though he was a big man, his waist was trim, his hips and thighs lean and slightly muscular. She blushed when he caught her staring.

"Are you still living on the estate?" she asked, her dazed mind recalling that he'd just mentioned putting in a pool. The Bufford mansion had had an Olympic-size swimming pool for as long as she could remember.

"I let Mike have it. He has a big family and needs the space. My place is in the country." He grabbed a sheet of paper and wrote out the directions for her. "Don't forget to tell Kelly to bring her swimsuit." He handed her the paper. His gaze was distant, cautious. "I'll see you then," he said.

"Yes, we'll be there," she said. Suddenly, there didn't seem to be anything else to say.

She turned for the door. "Could you tell me where I might find my mother?" she asked.

He started to say something, then changed his mind. "It'll be easier if I show you."

"You don't have to do that." But he was already walking toward her, holding in his hand the baffling production report he'd been studying before she'd arrived.

"I'm going in that direction anyway," he mumbled, not wanting her to think he was doing her a favor, then chastising himself for being so childish. He opened the door and motioned her through. She seemed to move past him reluctantly, as if there were something more she wanted to say. He could only hope she wouldn't drop any more bombshells at his feet for a while.

Scott ushered her through a maze of hallways, and Lucy was thankful for the escort, knowing she would have probably ended up in the men's room if left to find her way alone. Her mother was sitting at a battered desk in a cramped office when they found her, talking to a man with a clipboard. She spied Lucy and Scott, and her composure faltered for a split second. She wrote something on a slip of paper and handed it to the man before he went on his way.

"Here she is," Scott announced, nodding a brief

hello to Loretta before he turned back to Lucy. "Can you find your way out?"

"Sure, thanks," Lucy said, sounding more confident than she felt. She'd never realized the plant was so spread out. She stepped closer to her mother's desk. "Here's your medication. You forgot to take it this morning."

Loretta looked surprised. "You're right. But how did *you* know that?"

"I'm keeping up with it."

The woman shook her head sadly. "Lucy, don't you have anything better to do than count my pills every day to see that I'm taking them?"

"Not when it concerns your health. What's in the bag?" She pointed to a lunch sack on her mother's desk.

"Oh, that." Loretta reached for the bag, opened a desk drawer, and dropped it inside. "It's nothing."

Lucy opened the drawer and pulled out the sack, even though her mother protested. She reached in and pulled out what was inside. "Cupcakes, Mother?" she said accusingly.

"I'm hungry," Loretta whined. "You can't expect me to live off raw vegetables and tap water."

Lucy glared at her.

"Oh, for Pete's sake," Loretta said, taking the cupcakes and tossing them into the trash can.

Lucy smiled. "I'm proud of you."

Loretta seemed to forget food for a moment. "Not that it's any of my business, but what's going on between you and Scott?"

"Kelly and I are having dinner at his place tonight. We're going to tell her and Jeff the truth."

"'Bout time, if you ask me," Loretta said, eyeing the bag in the trash can. Another employee stepped into her cubbyhole and handed her a slip of paper. She checked it against a sheaf of papers on her desk. The phone rang.

"I'm leaving," Lucy said. Loretta nodded and smacked her lips together in a kiss as she snatched up the phone. Lucy started for the door, then retraced her steps, leaning over the trash can and plucking the cupcakes out before she went.

FOUR

Kelly was pleased to learn that Jeff Bufford's father had invited them for a cookout. She put on her best twill pants and a favorite sweater she'd bought with baby-sitting money. Lucy was determined not to dress up and have Scott think she was reading more into the invitation than he'd meant. She wore jeans and a long-sleeved cotton T beneath a flannel shirt.

"I've seen you dress better than that to take out the trash," Kelly muttered as they left the house.

"Mr. Bufford said it was casual," she told her daughter. "Besides, you're the one who is supposed to shine tonight," Lucy said.

Kelly finally seemed satisfied. "Jeffrey must really like me to have put his father up to this," she said. Her eyes sparkled with excitement, but Lucy suspected she was a bit nervous as well. She remembered the first time Scott had taken her to meet his parents. While they'd been civil enough, Aubrey's disparaging glances had told her she wasn't up to snuff in his book. Later, he'd forbidden them to see each other, so they'd been forced to seek more ingenious ways to be together.

"Jeff's parents are divorced, you know," Kelly said once they were on their way. "But they get along swell. 'Least that's what Jeff told me."

Lucy nodded. "That's good," she said, not knowing what else to say but feeling her daughter expected more. "Parents should be able to put their own feelings aside for the sake of their children."

She felt like a hypocrite the moment the words left her mouth. She and Scott certainly hadn't made any headway in that respect. All they'd done was gnaw on each other's last nerve from the moment they'd laid eyes on each other. She had to make him understand how important it was to put past hurts and disappointments aside and concentrate on their daughter's future. What addled her most was that Scott and his ex-wife were able to carry it off, when the two of them couldn't go five minutes in a room without one or the other's ire kicking up.

Perhaps she was expecting too much too quickly. After all, Scott had only just learned of Kelly's existence. For years he'd hated the woman his father had claimed walked out on him; now it was up to her to make him understand why she'd felt it necessary at the time. That would not happen overnight, of course, but if they worked at it, perhaps they could rekindle some of the trust and friendship they'd shared before. She was more than willing to try for Kelly's sake, she thought as she traveled down long-forgotten roads and noted some of the changes that had taken place in her absence.

"This is the road," Kelly said, interrupting her thoughts so suddenly that Lucy almost missed her turn.

"Jeez, Mom, what's with you today?" the girl asked,

giving a nervous giggle. "First you decide to dress like a bag lady, then you try to throw me through the windshield. Having a bad day, are we?"

"Something like that," Lucy muttered. "But don't worry, I won't embarrass you." Lucy found herself on a long stretch of road, heavily treed on either side with pine and cypress and live oak. She spotted the house from a distance, a sprawling redwood structure with a multitude of windows that backed up to the lake. The knot in her stomach grew as she drove closer, and it was the size of a fist by the time she pulled into the driveway.

She parked, and a gorgeous Irish setter loped from out of nowhere to greet them. "Wait to see if he's friendly," Lucy cautioned, having treated her share of dog bites in the emergency room.

"Oh, Mom, he's just a puppy," Kelly said, laughing.

Jeff opened the front door and hurried out, then scolded the dog for jumping on everyone. He stopped several feet away from Kelly and smiled shyly. "Glad you could make it. Did you bring your bathing suit?"

"Sure did," she said, holding up a canvas bag. "What's your dog's name?"

"Pepper. He's hyper." As if to prove it, the dog pounced on Lucy, who, now realizing he was friendly, laughed at the animal's overzealousness.

Jeff grabbed the dog by his collar. "Get down, Pepper! Watch it, Mrs. Odum, he'll slobber all over you."

The front door opened once more and Scott stepped out. His eyes automatically sought out his daughter, and it was all he could do to keep his emotions under control. He'd gotten only a quick look at her the other night, now he wished he could study her from every angle. But that might appear rude, and he didn't want to make a bad impression. "Where are your manners, Jeff?" he said, his inner turmoil masked by a welcoming smile. "Invite the ladies inside."

The boy laughed. "I'm trying, Dad, but Pepper won't leave them alone."

"Pepper, down!" Scott ordered, and the dog instantly hunkered down with his tail between his hind legs. He slumped under the nearest tree and lay his head on his front paws as though pouting. Lucy couldn't help but chuckle.

"Don't encourage him," Scott said.

Kelly looked at her mother. "That's the man you were with on Grandma's porch the other night," she whispered. "The one who made you cry."

"It's okay, honey. I'll explain it to you later."

"Come in," Scott said, fixing the animal with a stern look. "Before the beast grows bored sulking. Jeff hasn't had much luck training him, mainly because the dog can't sit still long enough to learn anything."

Lucy grinned. "Have you tried Ritalin? I've seen it work wonders on hyperactive kids."

Scott opened the door wider so they could enter. Up close, he could see that Kelly resembled him; she had his eyes and mouth. He was glad she had Lucy's pert nose. "Come in, Kelly," he said softly. "Make yourself at home."

Lucy and Kelly stepped into the living room and were instantly greeted by a yapping Yorkie wearing a pink ribbon. Scott chuckled. "Don't worry, her bark is definitely louder than her bite," he said. "She belongs to Jeff's mother, who's away at a convention."

"She's adorable," Kelly said, swooping her up in her arms. The Yorkie licked her jaw, and they all laughed. "What's her name?" the girl asked.

Jeff petted the dog. "Abby. Short for Abigail. My

mother paid a fortune for her and treats her like a real baby. She's sooo spoiled." He rolled his eyes as he said it. "She even has this little yellow raincoat to wear in case she has to tinkle in bad weather."

Lucy found herself smiling as she stroked the dog's silky fur. At the same time, she couldn't help but wonder why Scott's ex-wife preferred leaving her beloved pet with her ex-husband instead of a family member or friend. Not that it was any of her business, but she was curious nonetheless.

"I want a dog like this," Kelly said, snuggling the animal close.

"I doubt we could afford this breed," Lucy said, deciding the grooming alone would probably run a small fortune. At the same time, she realized now that they weren't living in an apartment with all the attached pet fees, they could afford a dog. "If you want a pet, you might have to settle on a mongrel from the animal shelter, but *only* if you clear it with Grandma first."

"Grandma will let me have a dog," the girl said. "She says yes to everything."

Lucy glanced at Scott. "It's all I can do to keep my mother from spoiling her rotten."

Scott was still studying Kelly curiously. When the girl suddenly looked up and found him staring, he glanced quickly at his son. "Why don't you two change into your bathing suits, and I'll get refreshments," he suggested.

"Come on," Jeff told Kelly. "I'll show you where you can change." Kelly passed the Yorkie to her mother, and the two teenagers disappeared into another part of the house.

Scott looked thoughtful. "She's beautiful," he said softly.

Lucy couldn't help but feel pleased. "Yes, I think so. She's also very bright, although the past couple of years she's been preoccupied with boys."

"At least we know she's normal."

"She wants to go to veterinary school. I keep reminding her how important her grades are."

"She looks like a *good* girl too," Scott said proudly. "I can tell you've raised her right."

Once again Lucy was pleased. "I've tried to involve her in a lot of activities," she said. "Dancing, Girl Scouts, youth programs at church. I've always felt if you keep children busy, there's less time for them to get into mischief."

Scott continued to gaze at Lucy, feeling as if there were something more he should say or do to show his appreciation. But what? Already, he was feeling guilty for not being there all those years.

"Don't," Lucy said.

He arched one brow. "Pardon me?"

She was surprised that she could still read him so clearly. "Don't put yourself on a guilt trip, Scott. Had you known about Kelly, I have every confidence you would have played a big part in her upbringing. That's just the kind of man you are. But you didn't know, so you have no reason to shoulder any blame."

"Did you bring your bathing suit?" he said, feeling a strong need to change the subject, at least temporarily. Later, when he was alone and his emotions weren't running so high, he would think about his feelings and responsibilities toward the girl.

Lucy shook her head. "I prefer to watch." Actually, she'd considered bringing her suit, but she'd finally decided against it for a variety of reasons. She already felt vulnerable toward Scott; this was certainly not the time to start disrobing, even if it was something as innocent as a swim.

There didn't seem to be anything else to say. Lucy quickly took in her surroundings, if only to keep from staring at him. The living room was neat, the overstuffed furniture done in shades of hunter green and rust. Framed photos had found their homes on end tables and a walnut library table that ran along one wall and gave the otherwise stark room a homey touch.

"Did you decorate the house?" she asked.

"Jeff and I picked out the furniture together," he said. "But I never really got around to buying pictures for the walls. I don't like a lot of clutter; it just collects dust."

"It looks nice," she said.

"Thanks." His dark eyes were sharp and assessing when they met her own, but less scornful than on previous occasions.

Once again the conversation lagged. They simply gazed at each other.

She noted the age lines about his mouth and eyes that concealed the once-youthful face yet emphasized a boldly handsome one.

He noted her delicately carved facial bones, the dusty flush of her cheeks. Her lips were full and generously curved, faintly rosy. Her windblown hair, shining like highly polished oak, made him wish he could bury his face in the lustrous mass and smell her fragrant shampoo.

"I was just going to make myself a cocktail," Scott said once the silence had become uncomfortable. "Can I get you something?"

"A glass of wine if you have it," she said. He nodded dutifully, and she was surprised by his civility. No doubt he was trying to be on his best behavior for the sake of the kids. She followed him into a massive kitchen with light oak cabinets and a work island surrounded by stools. Still holding Abby, she took a seat and watched him prepare the drinks. He pulled a bottle of white wine from the refrigerator, uncorked it, and poured.

"Just half a glass," she said. "I'm not much of a drinker. I suppose it has something to do with not wanting to follow in Darnel's footsteps."

He filled the glass half full and handed it to her. "Can't say that I blame you there." He remembered the times she'd come to him crying over her father's drunken sprees that sometimes lasted for days on end.

Lucy thanked him and took a sip. "You have a lovely home," she said, realizing they conversed like a couple of strangers now that they weren't talking about Kelly. There was no indication of their lengthy history together or the fact that they'd shared tense words that very afternoon. "How long have you lived here?"

"Seven or eight years now. My father thought I was crazy for buying the place when there was plenty of room at the house, but I wanted something of my own."

"I know the feeling," she said. "After I moved away, I rented a room near the school where I'd planned to study nursing. It felt so good having my own place, even if it wasn't much bigger than a closet. I bought a crib for Kelly from a secondhand store, and that's where we stayed for the next three years."

"I would have thought you could afford better," he said, then wished he hadn't when he saw her stiffen.

Lucy tightened her fingers around the stem of her wineglass, but she said nothing.

"I didn't mean for it to come out sounding like that," Scott said quickly, then wondered if perhaps he had. "From the way my father talked, you walked away with a bundle. I envisioned you living in one of those ocean-front high rises without a care in the world."

"That's not the way it was," she said crisply. "I had to live inexpensively while I attended nursing school; otherwise I would've had to work a full-time job as well. That wouldn't have given me any time with my baby."

"*Our* baby," he reminded her.

She met his look and wondered if he would be angry with her for the rest of her life. Why not blurt out the truth and be done with it, that Kelly would have been taken from her had she stayed. Aubrey Bufford didn't deserve to be protected after what he'd done to her. Then she reminded herself once again that she wasn't trying to protect Aubrey; she was looking after Scott's feelings. Aubrey might have treated her shamelessly, but he'd been Scott's father, perhaps even a hero figure, and she hated to take that from him. She knew firsthand what it was like being ashamed of the man who'd fathered you.

Scott noted the sadness in her eyes and cursed himself for being difficult. She was right. Every time she opened her mouth he found a way to jump down her throat. And it was so important that the evening go well for the kids' sakes! He and Lucy had to stop bickering and present a unified front if they were going to give the appearance of stability.

Nervously, he ran his hands through his hair, stood, and turned for the refrigerator. He opened the freezer door, plucked an ice cube from the bin, and plunked it into his drink. "Who cared for Kelly when you were in class?" he asked, trying to keep the topic a safe one, if there were such a thing.

The smile on her face told him it was an okay question to ask. "The lady who owned the place where we lived baby-sat while I was away. She was an older woman who absolutely adored babies and spoiled Kelly rotten. I couldn't afford to pay her much, but I don't think she did it for the money anyway." Lucy's eyes clouded and she took a sip of wine. "She died several years back. It came as quite a blow." She sighed, remembering how Mrs. Billingsly had become somewhat of a mother figure at one time, easing Lucy's overwhelming loneliness, seeing Kelly through colic and chicken pox and a whole slew of childhood illnesses.

"By the way," she said, trying to shrug off her sorrowful mood. "I have tons of pictures of Kelly growing up. You're welcome to the negatives."

"I'd like that." Scott regarded her thoughtfully. "So how come you didn't end up marrying a doctor like a lot of nurses do?" He knew he had no right to ask, but that didn't stop him. She was much too pretty to sit home on Saturday night, much too young to devote her life solely to her child and ignore her own needs, *if* in fact that's what she'd done.

"I didn't have much time for socializing, Scott. I was trying to raise a daughter and keep up with my studies and, later, my career." She wished there were a way to tell him how well she'd done in school and work without sounding as if she were bragging, but she was proud of her accomplishments.

"Being a trauma nurse, as I was for a number of years, takes a lot out of you," she added. "All I wanted to do at the end of the day was spend time with Kelly. I wasn't looking to meet men." She noted his pensive look. "Does that surprise you?"

"Nothing surprises me anymore, Luce."

The way he said her name conjured up images of earlier days, when he'd been gentle and loving, before his eyes had become hard, flat, and passionless, before his lips had become tight and grim and at times cynical. She did not want to be reminded of that young boy and wonder what would have become of them had she stood up to his father. "Please don't call me that."

Scott took a sip of his drink, eyeing her over the rim, seeing the play of emotions on her face. "Why not? Is it because it brings back memories?" He put his glass down and leaned against the counter, bringing his face closer to hers. Her eyes were gentle and contemplative, hardly what he expected from a woman his father had described as greedy and self-serving. He caught a whiff of her perfume and felt dizzy for a moment. It both surprised and annoyed him that she had that effect on him after all these years.

Lucy glanced up. Was this the same man she'd fallen head over heels in love with so many years ago? She was almost afraid of the changes in him, both physical and emotional. "We were just kids at the time," she said, feeling as though her oxygen supply were growing thin with each breath she took.

"Kids, maybe. But old enough to make a baby," he reminded her, his voice dropping an octave. "Do you remember the night Kelly was conceived?"

She almost shivered at the huskiness in his voice as she remembered what it had been like lying naked in his arms that first time, the sheen of his perspiration mingling with hers in the night air. They'd driven to the lake and had spread an old quilt on the grass, undressing each other in the light of a full moon. They'd been young and inexperienced and in no way prepared for lovemaking or parenthood.

"Yes, I remember," she said at last, her voice wistful. "Neither one of us used . . . um . . . protection that night. Later, when I found out I was pregnant, I was scared to tell you."

Actually, she'd been terrified, and she'd waited weeks before telling Scott. She had heard rumors about one of the girls in her class getting pregnant and having an abortion, but she knew in her heart there was no way she could destroy Scott's baby. What about his plans for college? she'd thought. Aubrey Bufford would have refused to pay for his son's education knowing there was a baby on the way. Lucy had worried herself into a frenzy.

Scott had been ecstatic when she'd finally worked up the nerve to tell him. He had hoped his father would accept Lucy into the family. Neither could have been more wrong. Aubrey had had big plans for his son, and they hadn't included marrying into the trashiest family in Shade Tree.

A sudden noise startled them so badly, they jumped. Kelly and Jeff hurried in, dressed in bathing suits.

"Mom, you've just got to see Jeff's computer," she said. "You can actually draw pictures on it. And he's got this superpowerful telescope and a color TV *with* cable and a stereo system to die for and . . ."

Lucy, a smile plastered to her face, listened politely as Scott shifted in his seat uncomfortably. "That's really nice, honey," she said for lack of knowing how else to respond. She couldn't afford any of these niceties for her daughter even though the girl had excelled in her computer courses in Atlanta.

Kelly regarded Jeff quizzically. "Well, are we going swimming, or are you just going to stand around like a bump on a log?"

He grinned. "Last one in the pool's a rotten egg." He and Kelly raced toward the sliding glass door off the living room, laughing heartily as they struggled to be the first one out. They'd barely closed the door behind them before there was the sound of splashing and more laughter.

"Well, now," Scott said once they were alone.

Lucy's look was cool. "Well, what?"

"I know what you're thinking."

"Oh?"

"You think I spoil Jeff, and maybe I do. It's just the only way I know to make up for not being with him all the time."

"We can't be with our children *all* the time, Scott."

"Then why the look of disapproval, Lucy?"

She averted her gaze. "Because I can't afford to give Kelly these things, and until now it didn't seem to make a difference to her."

"I can afford to give her anything she wants."

"I won't permit it." She spoke quietly but firmly. "I have very definite ideas on how she should be raised."

"I'm her father. Don't I have an opinion?"

"Not when it's contrary to everything I've instilled in her thus far."

He gazed back at her, his look penetrating. "Okay, Lucy, I'll back off for now. But only because I have no desire to make radical changes in our daughter's life. But don't expect me to pander to all your decisions. I'm not going to let the girl go without just because of your stubborn pride."

"Kelly has never *gone without*," Lucy said, feeling a bit indignant that he would even suggest such a thing. That didn't mean she hadn't given up necessities at times to see that their daughter had what she needed. Lucy had worn tattered uniforms to work and had bought her white nurses' shoes secondhand to save money for

Kelly's school clothes. Thankfully, Kelly had never felt she needed to wear designer clothes to fit in.

They were quiet for a moment, each of them caught up in thought.

In the background, Lucy could hear Jeff and Kelly splashing about the pool. She envied them. She could not remember a time in her life when she'd been able to enjoy her youth without worrying about things over which she'd had no control. Even when Scott had held her in his arms, she'd wondered what was going on at home, whether Darnel was drunk or if he was being mean to her mother.

Scott clasped his hands together and leaned forward on the counter. "So what do we do about *us*, Lucy?" he said. "Where do you and I go from here?"

That was the question of the hour, she realized. Where *did* they go from there? Would they be able to maintain the amicable relationship Scott had with his ex-wife, or would they constantly do battle with each other? She didn't have an answer for that.

"You know what I expect from you, Scott, in regards to Kelly."

"But what do *you* want?"

"Me?" She shrugged. "I don't know," she said, feeling anxious at the intensity of his gaze. She did know, but she wasn't about to confess it to him. "I suppose I want what every woman wants," she answered vaguely.

He arched one dark brow. "Most women want a home. Husband, family, love, the whole nine yards. Is that what you want?"

She sighed and wished they didn't have to be so serious when they weren't fighting. "I used to," she said. "But that dream died fifteen years ago, so I told myself I had no choice but to accept it and go on."

He surprised her by reaching for her hand and slipping it inside his shirt to lie against his chest. "Feel that?" he said. "My heart's still beating. I'm very much alive."

Lucy could feel her own heart thrumming in time with his. His flesh was warm and covered with crisp hair. She'd known him when he had very little chest and facial hair and had tried to hide the fact that it bothered him. She closed her eyes. If only things had not turned out the way they had. If only . . .

"Look at me, Lucy," he said.

She opened her eyes. His face was close, his look intense, galvanizing. She felt rooted to her seat.

"There was a time when I wished I'd never come out of the hospital. You've no idea what it was like, all those operations on my face, the physical therapy, sitting in a wheelchair and wondering whether I'd ever walk again. I *did* think of hiring a private investigator to find you, but my pride wouldn't allow it. If you could walk out on me while I was in a coma, how did I know you wouldn't walk out the next time things got tough?

"Then, one day I told myself I was going to have to put it all behind me and get on with my life. I was doing a pretty good job of it until you came back."

The last thing Lucy wanted to do was cry, but all at once she had tears in her eyes. "I'm sorry, Scott. It was not my intent to hurt you further when I came for my father's funeral. If I hadn't been convinced of your death, I would never have looked for your grave the day after my arrival." She tried to pull her hand free, but he held it in place.

"You looked for my grave?" he said. "What did you think when you were unable to find it?"

"I was confused, naturally. I thought maybe you'd

been cremated. I'd planned to call the business office but decided I could take care of all that once I moved back for good."

Her tears wrenched his gut. Still holding her hand over his heart, he got up and rounded the narrow counter. "Don't cry, Luce," he said gently. He pulled her hand free and draped a consoling arm across her shoulder. With his free hand he picked up her beverage napkin and dabbed her eyes. "Please don't cry. You know how I used to get crazy over that sort of thing when we were kids."

She remembered crying on his shoulder more than once as a kid, usually when Darnel's drinking had gotten out of hand. Like the White Knight she'd always dreamed of, Scott promised to take her away from it all as soon as they were married. But that promise had been broken by a drunk driver, and she'd had no choice but to rescue herself and her baby by running.

"I never got over you, Lucy," he said, his voice a mere whisper. She raised her face to his. Their gazes met, and for a moment it was like old times. Her heart took a crazy leap as he captured her lips with his.

The kiss started out innocently enough. Lucy felt him slip his tongue past her lips, and she felt an unwelcome surge of pleasure. She opened her mouth wide, eager to receive as much of him as she could. That seemed to be his undoing. His grip tightened. He backed her against the counter and pressed his body intimately against hers. As the kiss deepened, he ground his hardness into her belly. She moaned and arched against him, feeling as though each nerve ending was electrified. Her emotions and the heat in her belly were hard to resist. As she drank in the comfort of his nearness, his very essence, she was vaguely aware of the sounds coming from the pool area.

She realized she and Scott were on the verge of losing control. She pushed away and sucked in fresh air.

Scott was stunned by her hurtling back to logic and reason. "Why'd you push me away?" he asked, trying to catch his breath.

Lucy was trembling. "The children. They could walk in on us."

Reality returned like a shot of ice water in his veins. He stepped away from her, running a hand along his damp forehead, his upper lip, now beaded with perspiration. What could he have been thinking? "Sorry, I forgot."

"So what do we do now?" she asked. "Now that we know we're still . . . still attracted to each other." She knew she wasn't speaking out of turn. Her body ached for his touch, and she saw the smoldering flame in his eyes even now. Something in his manner jangled her insides; she felt cocooned in an invisible warmth. There was a deeper significance when their gazes met this time.

"Well, my first thought is to haul you off to my bedroom and make love to you until we both collapse," he said, drawing a blush from her. "But I know that's just my hormones talking, so I'm not about to do anything for which we might be sorry later."

As if to prove his point, he returned to his side of the counter. It wasn't the easiest decision he'd ever made, and it didn't stop him from wanting her. How could he want her so much when there were so many unanswered questions? But he knew in his heart if he ever got her in his bed, he'd never let her go. He suspected Lucy was as particular as he was these days. At least, he liked to think so.

She looked hurt. "What makes you think we'd be sorry if we made love?"

"We're not seventeen anymore, Luce. Like you said, we have children to think of."

She tried to hide her disappointment. It wasn't easy; she could still taste him on her lips, feel the imprint his hands had left on her. But she was not about to throw herself at Scott Bufford and risk making a fool of herself.

FIVE

By the time Kelly and Jeff came in from swimming, the burgers and hot dogs were ready. The glassed-in area was the size of a small gymnasium and offered everything. A kidney-shaped pool and hot tub took up most of the space, and they were surrounded by tables and expensive-looking lawn furniture.

The temperature was perfect; one would never have guessed it was winter outside the dome-shaped roof. Lucy suggested they eat at one of the tables near the pool instead of using the formal dining room. Everyone agreed. She suspected they were as tense as she was. As she carried out baked beans and cole slaw and a bowl of potato chips, Kelly and Jeff made a game of setting the table while Abby yipped at Lucy's heels and begged to be held.

She chuckled. "This dog is worse than a baby," she told Jeff.

He grinned. "I told you she was spoiled. Oh, and please don't use the D word in front of her. She thinks she's one of us."

Finally, it was time to sit down and eat. Lucy had no choice but to hold Abby in her lap. Thankfully, the animal curled into a ball and went to sleep.

"This is wonderful," Lucy said, once they'd filled their plates. "Makes me think of summertime. All we're missing are the mosquitoes."

"Jeff and I spend most of our time out here," Scott said. "It was well worth the expense."

She couldn't imagine the cost of building such a room, when all she longed for these days was an extra bathroom. It wasn't easy for three females to share one lavatory that was no bigger than a closet. Her mother had laughingly suggested they rent one of those portable potties and keep it in the backyard.

"Do you go out on the lake much?" Lucy asked Jeff.

He nodded. "All the time when the weather's warm. Dad taught me to ski when I was five years old."

"I'd like to learn," Kelly said.

Jeff nodded agreeably. "I can teach you." The two youngsters exchanged meaningful looks.

Lucy shifted nervously in her chair and shot Scott an anxious look. He glanced away quickly and went on eating his burger. They heard a scratching noise and saw that Pepper wanted in. He barked several times, waking Abby, who jumped from Lucy's lap and raced to the door. She stood there growling as menacingly as a five-pound furball could manage. Jeff started to get up.

"Don't let him in until we finish dinner," Scott said. "He'll be in the middle of the table eating out of our plates."

"I see you let him run loose," Lucy said. "Aren't you afraid he'll run away?"

"No," Scott and Jeff said in unison, then laughed.

"All he needs is someone to spend time with him," Kelly said. "How old is he?"

"Eleven months."

"He's still a puppy," Kelly replied. "I can help you train him."

Once they'd finished dinner, Jeff automatically started to gather the dishes. Scott cleared his throat. "Don't worry about that right now, son. Sit down, there's something I need to discuss with you and Kelly."

The two teenagers glanced at each other in surprise. "Have we done something wrong?" Jeff asked, reclaiming his seat.

Scott shook his head. "No, nothing like that. In fact, I'd say Lucy and I would be hard pressed to find better teenagers." Jeff looked relieved.

"Perhaps I should start first," Lucy said, noting Kelly looked confused and a bit anxious as well.

Scott held up both hands, as if surrendering. "I just don't want you to think I'm dumping the whole thing on you."

"I never said that," she protested. "Why would you even think it?"

"I know how you are, Luce. I offered to tell them myself, but if you insist on doing so, that's fine. I just don't want you to come back later and accuse me of not being supportive."

Kelly gave an embarrassed laugh. "Would you two please tell us what's going on?"

Lucy took a deep breath. "I owe you an apology, Kelly," she said. "For years you've begged me to tell you about your father."

Kelly nodded. "You *did* tell me about him. At least most of it," she said. She glanced around the table. "Why are you bringing it up *now*?" she asked, cutting her eyes in such a way that Lucy could tell she was embarrassed.

"Well—" Lucy hedged. "When I told you your father died in an automobile accident, I believed that to be true."

Kelly leaned forward on one elbow and cupped her eyes so that she was looking directly at her mother. "Yeah, so?"

"Then, when we came back for your grandfather's funeral, I learned I was mistaken."

Kelly frowned. "How can anybody *possibly* make a mistake like that?"

"My thoughts exactly," Scott muttered.

Lucy shot him a dark look, then turned her attention to her daughter. "You knew I didn't correspond with my family; in fact, I broke off all contact with friends and relatives after I left Shade Tree with the exception of my mother, to whom I sent birthday and Christmas cards every year. Still, she had no way of reaching me, no address. She wasn't able to tell me your father hadn't died, as I assumed."

Kelly's mouth fell open.

"Why didn't you give your mother your address?" Jeff asked Lucy, obviously caught up in the drama that was unfolding before him.

She looked at him. "My father drank. He often became mean. I didn't want him to know where Kelly and I were. I didn't want Kelly raised in that environment."

Jeff nodded as though it made complete sense. Scott stared at the salt and pepper shaker before him, his face blank.

"What does any of this have to do with my father?" Kelly demanded impatiently.

Lucy sighed heavily. "Your father isn't dead, Kelly. He's very much alive."

Kelly stared at her mother a full moment, eyes glistening with tears. "And you decided to tell me something like this *now*?" she said. "Couldn't you wait until—"

Scott reached for Kelly's hand, catching the girl by complete surprise. "Kelly honey," he said as gently as he could, "*I'm* your father."

The girl regarded him in mute disbelief. "You?"

"I hope you're not too disappointed."

She continued to stare at him. "But if you're my father, that makes Jeff and me—" She paused and looked at Jeff.

"Half brother and sister," he blurted out, his face turning beet-red.

Kelly pulled her hand free and slammed both palms on the table. "Oh, this is *great*!" she said, her own face a bright crimson. "Just great. I'm going out with a guy who happens to be my brother."

"*Half* brother," Lucy corrected her.

Jeff looked at Scott. "Why didn't you tell me, Dad?" he said.

"I only just learned of it myself, son."

Everyone looked at Lucy. She slid down in her chair and offered Jeff and Kelly a sheepish look. "I'm sorry. I had no desire to hurt either of you."

Kelly groaned. "Oh, jeez, what are the kids at school going to think?"

Jeff shook his head. "I dunno, Kelly, we might have to change schools. I don't think we did anything to be embarrassed about though. It's not like we walked around holding hands in the hall or something."

"You walked me to all my classes."

"That's no big deal. I can tell people I was trying to make you feel at home since you're my . . . my sister."

Kelly slid her chair from the table and walked toward the door leading out. She pushed it open and stepped outside, but not before Pepper lumbered through like a small pony.

"I'd better go after her," Lucy said, starting to rise.

"I'll talk to her, Mrs. Odum," Jeff offered, rising instead.

"Yes, go after her, Jeff," Scott urged, "and see if you can calm her down."

They were all so concerned about Kelly that they paid Pepper little notice. He jumped into Kelly's chair and plopped both paws on the table, knocking over bottles of ketchup and mustard and dill pickles. Lucy shrieked and tried to keep the mess to a minimum.

Scott leapt up and grabbed the dog by his collar. "Get *down*, Pepper!" he ordered, trying to pull the animal from the table. Pepper grabbed a hamburger between his teeth and took off.

Scott shouted a curse that would have embarrassed most truck drivers. "I'm going to wring your neck when I get my hands on you," he threatened.

The dog ran clear to the other side of the pool. Scott chased him around the pool, muttering threats under his breath while Lucy tried to gather up the rest of the food in case Pepper came back for seconds. She hurried inside. When she returned she found master and pet in a standoff. If she hadn't been so concerned about Kelly, she would have laughed.

"You're going to the animal shelter tomorrow, Pepper," Scott said. "I've had it with you, you sack of stupidity. You bag of worthless bones."

"No wonder he won't come to you," Lucy said. "All

you do is yell at him. Haven't you heard the old saying that you can catch more flies with honey than vinegar?"

"Let's see *you* get him over here."

Lucy called the dog softly. "Come here, Pepper," she said sweetly. "Come here, boy." The dog swallowed the hamburger in one gulp, then stood and wagged his tail. Still, he hesitated. "Come on, honey, I'm not going to hurt your feelings like Mr. Meanie here. Back away, Scott, you're making him nervous."

"That's because he knows I'm going to drown him in the lake once I get my hands on him."

She shot him a look. "You don't think he can understand you, but, believe me, he knows exactly what you're saying." She frowned at him, then made her way closer to the dog, skirting the edge of the pool and kneeling on one knee. "Come on, Pepper," she said, making kissy sounds with her lips that had Abby running in circles and yapping wildly. "Mean old daddy isn't going to hurt you. I won't let him."

The dog, still watching Scott from the corner of his eye, slowly made his way around the pool toward Lucy. Finally, he stopped within inches of her.

"Grab his collar so he can't get away," Scott muttered through closed lips as though imitating a ventriloquist.

"Only if you promise not to yell at him anymore," she said.

"I just want to put him out."

Lucy stroked the dog's sleek coat and praised him for being so good. Finally, she closed her fingers around his collar. "That's a good boy," she said sweetly.

"I've got you now, buster," Scott said, lunging for the animal.

Lucy was not prepared for Scott's sudden rush or the

dog's mad dash to escape his owner. Instead of going back the way he'd come, Pepper took a flying leap into the pool. Her fingers still clamped tight around his collar, Lucy went in right behind him.

She came up coughing and sputtering. "I can't believe you did that!" she yelled at Scott.

"Me? I didn't do a damn thing. Mr. Loose Screws over there pulled you in."

Lucy glanced around and saw the animal paddling toward the other end of the pool. He climbed out and shook his red coat, droplets of water fanning out around him like a sprinkler gone haywire.

Trying to swallow a chuckle, Scott leaned forward and offered his hand. "Swim over here, and I'll help you out." He'd obviously forgotten his anger toward the dog in his attempt to keep a straight face.

It was the first time Lucy could remember him looking at her without frown lines between his eyebrows. In fact, he looked like he might break out into hearty guffaws at any minute. "Forget it, Scott. I'd sooner drown."

He tried to look sympathetic and failed miserably. "I'm sorry, Luce, but that's not going to be easy with you standing in three feet of water." She glared back at him beneath a mop of wet hair. "How was I supposed to know the dumb animal was going to jump in the water and take you with him?" he insisted, the corners of his lips twitching despite his best efforts to remain solemn.

"That's not funny," she said, praying her mascara wasn't running down her face. She'd finally made it to the side and reached up to take Scott's hand. His smug look was her undoing. She grasped his hand tightly and yanked with all her might.

At first he looked surprised. He muttered a curse and tried to regain his balance but was not quick enough.

The next thing either of them knew, he was in the water beside her.

When he came up for air he looked angry. "What the hell did you do that for?" he demanded, reaching into his back pocket for his wallet. He looked inside and found his money wet, not to mention everything else that wasn't coated with plastic. He dropped them on the edge of the pool and regarded her, hands on hips.

"You thought the situation quite funny a minute ago," she said. "Now that you're all wet, you've suddenly lost your sense of humor."

The frown on his face died the minute he noted the shirt she wore, very wet and literally plastered to her breasts. He felt his mouth go bone-dry at the sight of her erect nipples, felt something stir below his belt. He raked his hair from his face and gazed at her as though seeing her for the first time. He clenched his fists together, then unclenched them. He didn't realize he was gritting his teeth until he felt the ache of his jaw muscles.

"This is . . . very awkward," he managed to get out, trying to sound distant and aloof when his entire body strained to get closer. He didn't even hear the light tap on the glass door, and he paid no mind to Abby's sudden yapping.

"Hmmm." Lucy seemed to ponder what he'd said as she gazed at a spot directly over his shoulder. "If you think *this* is awkward, just wait till you get a load of the woman staring at us through your glass doors."

Scott glanced over his shoulder about the same time the sliding glass door whisked open and a petite redhead stepped out, sending Abby into a tizzy. "Excuuuse me," she said, arching one pert brow. "I rang the doorbell, but nobody answered."

Scott offered the woman an embarrassed smile.

"Amy, what on earth are *you* doing here? You're supposed to be in Chicago."

The woman reached for her Yorkie, gave her a big hug and kiss, and stepped closer. "I got in a day early and stopped by on my way back from the airport. I figured after a week of keeping Jeff, you'd be ready to send him back." She paused and glanced at Lucy, then back at Scott. "Sorry to barge in on your party."

"No problem," Scott said. He put his hands flat on the side of the pool and hefted himself up, then reached for Lucy. "That damn Pepper pulled Lucy into the pool."

"Oh?" She glanced in the dog's direction, then noted Scott's own wet clothing with a wry smile. "And so big brave you jumped in to save her."

"Something like that."

Amy held her hand out to Lucy. "Hi, I'm Jeff's mother, Amy Bufford. I don't know why Scott insists on keeping that animal. He's such a nuisance."

Lucy shook her hand. "Lucy Odum," she said.

Amy glanced at Scott. "*The* Lucy?" she said. He nodded gravely. "Very interesting," she replied. "Is Jeff around?"

"He's here somewhere," Scott said, "but he has company. Would it be okay if I brought him home later?"

"Sure. I just missed the little rascal, you know?" She turned to Lucy once more. "It was nice meeting you, Miss Odum. I've heard so much about you, I feel I've known you all my life."

"Nice to meet you," Lucy said, feeling utterly ridiculous as she dripped water everywhere. "I hope our next meeting will be in drier surroundings."

"I can see myself out, Scott," Amy said, then made

her way through the glass doors, whispering baby talk and cuddling her pet as she went.

Scott and Lucy stared at each other for a moment, each of them silent.

"I feel like an idiot," she confessed at last. "The woman probably won't allow her son near me after today."

Scott chuckled. "Amy doesn't get rattled easily. Where do you think our children have run off to?"

"Heaven only knows. You think we should look for them?"

"They have a lot to think about. They'll come back when they're ready." He glanced at the dog, still sitting at the edge of the pool, alert for the slightest move in his direction. "I'm still not finished with you, Pepper." He looked at Lucy. "Want a towel?"

"That would be nice."

"Follow me."

They kicked their shoes off before going inside. Scott led Lucy into a masculine-looking bedroom and pulled a terry-cloth robe from the closet. Put this on, and I'll stick your clothes in the dryer." He motioned toward a door, and she stepped inside a bathroom papered in hunter green and burgundy. It smelled faintly of his aftershave.

She couldn't resist touching the plush bath towels and polished-cotton shower curtain. She peeked into his medicine cabinet, then closed it when she decided she was snooping. She had no right to touch his personal belongings, even if it was the only way she knew to feel close to him again.

When Lucy came out she found Scott dressed in shorts and a shirt and sneakers without socks. He grabbed her clothes and headed for the kitchen. "You want a cup of coffee?"

"Sure. Why don't you make it while I finish clearing the table?"

She hurried out to the pool area and was disappointed to find Kelly and Jeff hadn't yet returned. Pepper, who obviously thought he was safe now, was dozing on a nearby chaise longue. He raised his head when he saw her, yawned wide, and closed his eyes once more.

By the time Lucy had carried everything in and wiped the table, Scott had poured two cups of coffee. They sat down at the island and sipped in silence for a moment.

"I'm sorry Pepper pulled you into the pool," he said. "I hope nothing was ruined. I'll pay for any damages."

"Don't worry. I don't own much that can be harmed by good old H_2O."

They both smiled, and for a moment the tension was gone between them.

"Tell me about Amy," she said, taking another sip of her coffee.

His eyes became hooded. "What about her?"

"What's she like?"

"You just saw for yourself."

"First meetings don't really tell you a whole lot about a person." She paused. "I sort of got the impression she knew about me."

"Yeah, I told her about us when she and I first met." He paused and took a sip of his coffee. "Amy and I have been divorced a long time. I don't dabble into her affairs, and she stays out of mine. That's not to say we don't like each other, because we do, and we both share Jeff's best interests, of course. I couldn't ask for a better mother for my son."

"How come she never remarried?"

Scott shrugged. "You'd have to ask her that. I haven't a clue."

"Maybe she's still in love with you."

His eyes narrowed briefly. "She divorced *me*, it wasn't the other way around." He shrugged. "Who knows, maybe she's being cautious."

"Ten years is a long time to be cautious."

Scott wondered why Lucy was so curious about his ex-wife. "Amy is very devoted to her career," he said. "For the sake of our son, I'm glad she doesn't hop into bed with every man that comes along. Surely you can appreciate that in a mother. Being one yourself," he added.

Lucy knew he was waiting for her to agree with him, waiting for her to say yes, she had put her entire life on hold for her daughter, which, in fact, she had. But it was for that reason she remained quiet and was rewarded with another one of his frowns. Finally, she couldn't resist teasing him just a little.

"Well, you know me. I say go for the gusto!"

He almost choked on his coffee.

The front door opened, and Kelly stepped through with Jeff right behind her. They caught one look at Lucy in the oversized bathrobe and came to an abrupt halt. "What happened to you?" Kelly said. "Why is your hair all wet?"

"Pepper pulled her into the pool," Scott replied. "You should have seen it, the funniest thing I've ever witnessed in my life."

"Why is *your* hair wet, Dad?" Jeff asked. Scott dropped his smile.

"I pulled your dad into the pool for laughing at me," Lucy replied.

"Wow, I guess we really missed out," Jeff said, as though trying to lighten the moment.

Scott stood, rounded the island, and regarded Kelly

for a moment. It was obvious she'd been crying, and he was proud that his son had been there for her to talk to.

"I know all this came as a shock to you, Kelly," he said gently. "It did to me too. But I consider myself very fortunate to have you for my daughter."

Kelly's eyes misted, and she stepped closer. Scott wrapped his arms around her. Jeff patted his father on the back, and Lucy had to look the other way because the tears were literally streaming down her face.

"Don't worry, Kelly," Jeff said. "I'll clue you in on all his weak spots. Before you're finished with him, he'll be putty in your hands."

She laughed despite the tears in her eyes. "Maybe he'll let me start dating earlier than my mom."

"Not!" Scott replied sternly, and they all laughed.

"Would you excuse me?" Lucy said, hurrying toward the bathroom.

Scott's gaze followed her. He could see that she was upset. "Why don't you guys grab dessert, and I'll check on Lucy," he suggested. He hurried toward the bathroom and knocked on the door. "Lucy? Let me in."

She unlocked the door and reclaimed her seat on the side of the tub, where she was crying into a tissue.

Scott stepped into the room and closed the door. "Are you okay?"

"I'm fine," she said. "I just got a little emotional is all." She was not about to tell him how bad she felt because her daughter had had to wait until she was practically grown to meet her father. No doubt Scott would gloat forever.

Scott lowered the toilet lid and sat down, then took one of Lucy's hands in his. "I'll do everything in my power to make up for the lost years." He noted her despair and knew she was not putting on an act. Much to his surprise, he felt saddened. She looked so pathetic in his bathroom with her wet hair and red eyes that he wanted to take her in his arms and kiss away the hurt.

But he couldn't. He knew how vulnerable he was to her, and until he got a grip on himself he had to be very careful. Besides, she had no one but herself to blame for staying away so long, no matter what her reasons.

He stood and squared his shoulders, and when he spoke there was no indication of the battle waging inside him. "Why don't you dry your eyes and come have dessert with us."

Lucy nodded and watched him turn for the door. She wished he could let go of the past just once and take her in his arms.

Loretta was watching TV and eating fat-free nachos with salsa when they came in. She wore spongy pink curlers in her hair and a garish tangerine kimono of cheap material. Lucy wished she could afford to buy nice things for her mother.

Kelly said good night, disappeared into the bedroom, and Lucy fell in an exhausted heap on the sofa.

"How'd it go?" Loretta asked.

"All the secrets are out of the woodwork. Kelly was upset at first. I think she and Jeff were getting close fast. Anyway, she seems okay now." Lucy paused. "By the way, I met Scott's ex-wife, Amy."

"What'd you think of her?"

"She seems nice enough. I find it hard to believe she hasn't remarried in all these years."

"Word has it she's still carrying a torch for him."

"Or maybe she's being cautious," Lucy said, wanting to give the woman the benefit of the doubt.

"Everyone knows he never really loved her."

"So why'd he marry her?"

"I shouldn't have to tell you that. The boy was crushed when you left. Not only did Amy teach him to walk again, she listened to his problems. She's a few years older than Scott, you know. I'm sure he looked to her for guidance. Then, before long he started feeling obligated to her. At least that's the way I figured it. Before they split up he bought her a very nice house."

"So why do you suppose *he* hasn't remarried?"

Loretta shrugged. "It wouldn't surprise me if he's waiting for her to find someone first. Maybe then he'll feel free to seek another mate. Who knows what he's thinking."

"Mother?"

"Yes?"

She pointed to the bag of nachos. "Just because it says *fat free* doesn't mean you're allowed to eat the whole thing."

Loretta put the bag aside. "Sorry, but that leftover cabbage soup didn't really do the trick. I could go for some fried okra and sliced tomatoes about now. Or how about a nice macaroni and cheese pie. Heavy on the cheese."

"Try to think of something other than food."

Loretta was quiet for a moment. "Like what?"

"Like how much weight you've already taken off. And how good you'll feel when you take off the rest."

Loretta sighed heavily. "I'm not really heavy, you know. I'm just big-boned."

Lucy's expression remained deadpan.

"And besides that, obesity runs in my family. It's in my genes. Just look at your aunt Abeline and cousin Martha. Why, they're as big as school buses."

"And they both have health problems. Besides, do you want to look like them?"

"No, of course not. Forget I said anything about fried okra or macaroni and cheese. I wouldn't touch the stuff with a ten-foot pole."

Lucy was still pondering the relationship between Scott and Amy when she went to bed. She also wondered how Amy would react when she learned Kelly was Scott's daughter. Would she resent the girl? Lucy worried about it until she drifted off to sleep.

On Monday, Scott called Lucy at work and asked if he could take Kelly out for pizza. "I certainly don't mind," Lucy told him, "but why don't you call Kelly at home about three-thirty and see if she's free?"

It had been raining steadily all day and hadn't let up when Lucy left work shortly after five. She arrived home fifteen minutes later to find her mother and Kelly setting pots and bowls around the house to catch the leaks.

"Danged roof leaks worse every year," Loretta muttered, setting an empty water pitcher at the entry to the hall.

"Have you thought about having it repaired?" Lucy asked.

"Of course I've thought about it, but once I started checking prices, I knew there was no way I could afford it." The doorbell rang and Loretta hurried to open it. "Oh, Scott, it's you. Come in, come in. Be careful, everything's wet."

"Good God," he said, noting the numerous pots scattered about the room. "You've got more leaks than the *Titanic*."

Lucy was embarrassed to have to tell him they

couldn't afford to have the roof fixed—the last thing she wanted from him was pity—so she decided to stretch the truth just a bit.

"Mother's been trying for weeks to get someone out here to make repairs to the roof, but you know how hard it is to find good help." He nodded as though in complete agreement.

"And then they want an arm and a leg to do it," Loretta said. "Be cheaper to move."

Scott went right on nodding as though he understood exactly where they were coming from, and Lucy was tempted to ask him when he'd last slept under a leaky roof. But she knew that would only start another squabble between them, and they didn't need it. Besides, she had decided to be as nice to him as she possibly could, despite his feelings toward her.

"Hold on a second," she said, "and I'll tell Kelly you're here." Lucy hurried toward the bedroom she shared with her daughter and tapped on the door. "Scott's here, honey."

Scott was standing on a chair, inspecting one of the leaks, when she returned. "What are you doing?" she asked.

He stepped down. "Just trying to see how bad it is." He turned to Loretta. "I know a good roofer who wouldn't charge much to make your repairs."

"I don't care how good he is," Loretta said. "As long as he's cheap."

Scott smiled. "I'll have to check with him and get back to you."

Kelly stepped out wearing jeans and a sweater. "I'm ready," she said a bit shyly. She glanced at Lucy. "I did all my homework."

Lucy nodded and followed them to the door. Although she was pleased Scott was taking an interest in the girl, she suddenly felt left out. She told herself she was being silly. "You two have a good time," she said, trying to hide her envy.

Once they were gone, Lucy and Loretta dined on chili made with ground turkey, and cheese toast with low-fat cheese and thin slices of diet bread. Loretta admitted she couldn't tell the difference. Afterward, Lucy baked two apples and put a scoop of low-fat vanilla ice cream on each one for dessert.

"Too bad it's raining," Loretta said. "I was actually looking foward to our walk."

Lucy tried not to smile. She suspected her mother was thrilled over the prospect of hitting the sofa as soon as they cleaned the kitchen. "I have an idea," she said. "Remember those old forty-fives you used to play when I was a kid?"

It was one of the few good memories Lucy had growing up, she and her mother dancing to Elvis Presley and Chuck Berry and a number of old tunes. It was also one of the few times Loretta had seemed happy and youthful. "Do you still have them?"

Loretta offered her a blank look. "They're somewhere around here. Probably in the attic."

"I'll look for them after we clean up."

"What are you planning to do with them?"

"We can dance our calories away."

Once the kitchen had been restored to order, Lucy carried a chair to the hall, climbed up on it, and tugged the small cord that pulled open the attic door. A set of stairs opened before her, letting out the smell of mothballs and dust. Loretta, holding the stairs in place, cautioned Lucy as she climbed up.

"Be careful," she said. "I don't know how safe the floor is up there."

At the top, Lucy tugged a string, and a naked bulb flashed on. The attic wasn't much larger than a walk-in closet, and, thankfully, there were less than a dozen boxes up there. Lucy checked several and smiled when she noted her mother had saved all her school papers and other memorabilia. She thought it might be fun to go through them with Kelly one day.

She found the box of records, 33's and 45's still sheathed in their original jackets. She didn't look at them until she'd carried them down and closed the attic door once more.

"Your stereo still works, doesn't it?" she asked her mother as she set the box on the coffee table and started going through the records. She glanced at the old TV and stereo console that had to be almost as old as she was.

"Oh, yes. I could never afford those fancy cassette and CD players. Melvin Henderson over at the Fix and Repair Shop has kept it in tiptop shape for me."

"I'm surprised he could find the parts. They certainly don't manufacture them anymore." She sifted through the 45's, through records by Frank Sinatra, Chubby Checker, Nat "King" Cole, Johnny Mathis, Jerry Lee Lewis, and, of course, Elvis, just to name a few.

"Oh, Melvin saves everything. And what he doesn't have he can usually find, as long as you aren't in a hurry."

"Let's warm up to *Jailhouse Rock*," Lucy said, handing her mother the small record. While Loretta concentrated on putting it on, Lucy rolled the rug back and moved a chair out of their way. The record dropped onto the turntable, and the needle settled gently in the groove. Lucy kicked off her sneakers and told her mother to do the same. Static filled the room before the song began, then Elvis began singing about going to a party in the county jail.

"Let's twist," Lucy said, grabbing her mother's hand. Loretta laughed and started to dance. They'd worked up a light sweat by the time they put on a Chubby Checker song. Lucy had tied up her shirttail, showing off plenty of midriff, and had grabbed a rubber band to pull up her hair.

By now they were experts and showing off a little bit. Lucy was in the process of a sexy grind that had Loretta, who was trying to moonwalk like Michael Jackson, in stitches. Neither of them saw Scott and Kelly walk through the front door.

Scott came to an abrupt halt the minute he spied Lucy's bare belly and gyrating hips. His body reacted immediately; his mouth went dry and his stomach took a dive. He watched her hold her nose as though she were going underwater, then sucked in his breath sharply as she began a provocative shimmy. "I should probably go," he told Kelly, trying to make himself heard over the music.

Kelly, blushing profusely, called out to her mother, but the music was too loud. Lucy had just started dancing the funky chicken, when Loretta happened to glance up from what looked like a one-sided version of the jitter-bug.

"Oh, my," her lips mouthed. She stopped dancing immediately.

Lucy, eyes closed and deafened by the music, was oblivious of her audience as she returned to a bump and grind that spoke volumes to her audience. She didn't open her eyes until the music stopped. She saw the look on her mother's face and turned. "Oh, Lord," she said upon seeing Scott and her daughter. "How long have you been standing there?"

"A while," Kelly replied, her cheeks a bright red.

Scott tried to talk around the lump in his throat. "Just long enough to realize you missed your calling in life," he managed to say. "You ever thought of joining the burlesque?"

Lucy was determined not to let him see how embarrassed she was. "Nothing wrong with having a little fun now and then, is there? It's not healthy to take life so seriously."

He knew she was referring to him. "I believe in having a good time," he said. "As long as I take care of my responsibilities first."

Which was his way of saying she didn't, of course. She hid her irritation by planting a bright smile on her face. "Oh, well, you don't have to remind me about responsibilities," she said in a singsong voice. She wanted to remind him that she'd been a single parent at seventeen, that she'd managed to get her education *and* care for her daughter without his help, but she knew there was no way to say it without turning their conversation into another boxing match.

Instead, she turned her attention to her daughter. She noticed the girl was holding something inside her jacket. "What have you got there?" she asked curiously.

"A puppy." Kelly pulled out a tiny creature with silver and black fur. "He's a Yorkie like Abby. Dad had him flown in from Jacksonville as a surprise. I named him Champ because he's got this championship bloodline and all. Isn't he the most adorable thing you ever saw?"

Lucy felt the smile grow stiff on her face. "Adorable," Lucy agreed. She glanced at Scott. "I don't know what to say."

"I hope you don't mind," he said. "I saw how much Kelly liked Abby, so I couldn't resist. He's had all his shots and has been wormed. I've got a bag of puppy food in the trunk of my car."

"Seems you thought of everything."

As though sensing the sudden tension in the air, Loretta piped up. "Come on, Kelly honey. We need to find a box for Champ to sleep in. I'm sure I've got something around here."

The girl nodded enthusiastically and followed her grandmother out of the room.

Scott and Lucy stared at each other in silence. He raked one hand through his hair. "I sort of get the impression you wish I hadn't bought her the dog," he said.

"It would have been nice if you'd said something first, so I could clear it with my mother. After all, this is *her* house. She may not appreciate having a puppy around."

"I didn't think Loretta would mind," he said. "I'll take responsibility for any damage he causes."

"Did it ever occur to you to ask *me* before you went out and bought him?"

"Look, I just wanted to do something nice for Kelly, okay? I would never have done it if I'd known you were going to make a big deal out of it. If you don't want her to have the damn dog, just say the word, and I'll send him back."

"So I can look like the villain?"

"You were going to get her a pet anyway. I heard you tell her."

"Yes, but *after* I made it okay with my mother. I wouldn't have just marched in here with a dog without her approval, and I certainly wouldn't have spent that kind of money on a pet."

He started for the door. "You confuse me, Lucy," he said. He opened the door and stepped out on the porch. She followed. "You know what your problem is?" he said. "You're jealous."

She almost laughed. "Jealous. Of whom? Of what?"

"You've had Kelly all to yourself these past fifteen years, and it burns the hell out of you that you've got to share her with somebody else."

"That's crazy. I want Kelly to be happy."

"She *is* happy. She had a wonderful time tonight. But you're bound and determined to blow it for her. Well, go ahead, but I'm not going to stand around and watch. And I'm sure not going to apologize to you every time I do something nice for my daughter."

He turned and walked toward his car without another word. He started the engine and pulled away, and as Lucy watched him drive off into the night, she felt an ache take hold deep inside her.

SIX

Two days later Scott was waiting for Lucy when she finished work. He had parked his car next to hers and was leaning against it as though he had all day.

"What are you doing here?" she asked, noting how good he looked in a rust-colored cotton shirt and faded jeans. The shirt, open at the collar, revealed thick black chest hair that made her long for a closer look.

"I want to show you something," he said. "Hop in." He opened the door on the passenger side for her. When she hesitated, he became insistent. "It won't take long."

She climbed into his Lincoln and put on her seat belt as he rounded the car and climbed in on the other side.

"What is it?" she asked.

"Be patient, you'll see."

He drove for a distance in silence. He couldn't help but notice how prim she looked in a sage and oatmeal print suit. He remembered how she'd looked doing the shimmy in her mother's living room.

"About the other night," he began. "I guess I should

have discussed buying a pet for Kelly with you ahead of time."

She glanced at him and saw that he was sincere. "It's okay. My mother is as thrilled as Kelly is to have a puppy in the house." She paused. "I suppose I overreacted. Maybe you're right. Maybe I am just a wee bit jealous. I've never had to share Kelly until now. It takes some getting used to."

"I'm not trying to take her from you, Luce," he said. "I just want to reassure her that I didn't purposefully avoid her all those years."

"She knows that. We had a long talk the other night after we left your place. She asked about the rest of your family, specifically, your mother."

"How *is* my mother?" he asked.

"About the same."

He looked amused. "Meaning she complains a lot."

"I don't think she does it on purpose. She's bored and has nothing to do. I'm trying to get her more involved with the other patients, but she thinks our programs are silly."

"That sounds like the mother I know and love," he said, smiling. "Tell her if she thinks they're so silly, she should try to come up with a few suggestions of her own."

Lucy pondered it. "I might just do that. If I can get her out of that blasted wheelchair."

His smile faded. "She has arthritis in her feet and ankles."

Lucy sighed. "Scott, you know that simply isn't true."

He looked thoughtful. "Okay, so maybe it's not as bad as she claims. Maybe the wheelchair makes her feel special. What's the harm?"

"The longer she uses it, the harder it's going to be for us to get her up and about. She's in perfect physical health save for a few minor aches and pains that come with aging. She should be strolling the grounds or going out with friends." She started to say more, then decided against it.

"What?" he said. "I can tell you haven't had your full say."

"I don't know why your mother is in Restful Valley to begin with. She doesn't need assisted care."

"You don't know what we've been through with her, Lucy," he said tersely. "You weren't here. She was so lonely after my father died. She begged Mike to move his family in. Mike's poor wife ended up playing nursemaid twenty-four hours a day. I was having to drive her to her doctor in Savannah twice a week for one thing or another because she insists all the doctors here are quacks. The only reason she puts up with the doctor at Restful Valley is that he's a member of the Yacht Club and she approves of his lineage."

"Maybe these small illnesses are the only way she knows to get attention."

"So you're saying she's a hypochondriac? What about all those headaches?"

Lucy looked out the window at the passing scenery. "I've seen her charts, Scott. I hope my health is half as good when I'm her age."

"So why was Restful Valley so eager to give her a bed when we applied?"

"I think you know the answer to that."

Scott was quiet. Of course he knew. The Buffords had invested heavily in the nursing home. In another year they would start building an enormous retirement community on the adjoining acreage that would include a clinic. That would probably be more suitable for his mother, but he had no idea what to do with her in the meantime. He'd hired nurses and companions for her when she still lived at home, but she'd fired every one of them.

"I'm tired of this secrecy," Lucy announced after they'd ridden in silence for a time. "When are you going to tell me where you're taking me?"

"How about right now?" He turned into a neighborhood of older homes and pulled in front of a massive Victorian that was presently being painted a soft cream color.

"Why are we stopping here?" Lucy asked.

"This is what I wanted to show you." He got out of the car and came around to her side to help her out. "Come on," he prodded, taking her hand. She stepped from the car, and he led her up a small walk to the wraparound porch. Lucy stared at the balustrade and fretwork while Scott fumbled in his pocket for a key.

Once he opened the front door, he motioned her in, and Lucy found herself standing in a large living room with wood floors and what looked to be ten-foot ceilings with ornate dentil molding. "Wow? Who lives here?"

Scott regarded her curiously. "I thought you might like to."

"Me?" A hand flew to her chest. "Are you crazy, I can't afford a place like this."

"The man who owned it owed my father a lot of money. When he died, the house was willed to our family as recompense for the loan. My brother owns half of it, but he's willing to make me a good deal, since I'm such a nice guy."

"I still don't get it," Lucy said.

"I'd like to deed the place over to you and Kelly," he

said. "Loretta can live here too. There's a separate apartment on the third floor."

Lucy shook her head. "I can't live here, Scott," she said. "First of all, I'm not going to let you buy me a house, and, secondly, I couldn't afford the utilities. Why, it's got to have over four thousand square feet. Could you imagine me trying to heat and cool the place?"

"I'll help with all that, Lucy," he said, waving it off.

"No you won't. Because I won't let you."

"Kelly's my daughter too. I want to see that she has a nice home."

"She *already* has a nice home. I'm sorry if you don't share that sentiment."

He shoved his hands into his pockets. She was a proud woman, and he didn't want to insult her. Still, he had to point out the truth. "Your mother's place is falling apart, and you know it. The roof is about to cave in, and God only knows what condition the wiring and plumbing are in."

"Then we'll make repairs as we can afford them." Lucy started for the door. "I'm going to the car."

"You're not even going to look at the rest of the house?"

"No."

"Wait a minute," he said, rushing ahead of her and standing in front of the door so she couldn't pass. "Think, Lucy. How much would you say you've spent on Kelly in the fifteen years you've had her?"

She frowned. "How should I know? She's my daughter, I didn't keep a running account."

"I'm willing to bet it's more than it would cost me to put you in this house." He paused and held his hands out. "See, this is my way of making up for not being there all those years, for not sharing in the responsibility."

"It wasn't your fault you weren't there, and you *are* taking responsibility now. Inviting her to dinner the other night was the best thing you could have done for her. Besides, I don't want you to give Kelly a lot of material things just because you can afford it. I don't like the idea of you paying a fortune for some championship dog when we can just as easily take Kelly to the animal shelter."

"So that's why you were ticked off at me," he said.

She didn't answer right away. How could she make him understand, a man who'd grown up with all the advantages?

"Scott, I wasn't able to shower Kelly with gifts when she was growing up, but it never seemed to matter because she always had the necessities, and she knew she was deeply loved. If you start handing her everything on a silver platter, she won't appreciate the smaller pleasures in life."

"Are we going to go to war every time I try to do something for my daughter?" he asked.

"She's my daughter too. And, as I said before, I have very definite ideas about how I want her raised."

He frowned. "And what about me? Don't I have anything to say about it?"

"Of course you do. But I'm not about to let you undo everything I've taught her."

"Is that what you think I'm trying to do?"

"Not intentionally. But you'll have to agree our upbringings were radically different. You've always had everything you ever wanted."

He leaned closer. "That's where you're wrong, Luce. If I had everything I'd always wanted, you and I would be happily married with about six kids now. But not a damned thing happened my way. I ended up with a woman I didn't love." He suddenly looked angry. "Do you know what it's like to go to bed with someone you don't love, Lucy? To pretend that person is somebody else? To actually call that person by the wrong name?"

Lucy covered her ears, unable to listen to any more. "Please take me home now, Scott. I don't want to listen to—"

He grabbed her wrists. "Oh, yes, you do. It's time you knew the truth. I was so damn pathetic, it's a wonder Amy would even have me. At first I thought it was pity. Finally, I realized the poor woman actually loved me." He shook his head sadly, but his eyes were bitter. "But no matter how hard she tried, how hard *I* tried, I couldn't stop thinking of you."

There were tears in his eyes now. "I thought after Jeff was born things would be different, but they weren't. I couldn't get you out of my mind. Don't you think that's scary, Lucy? Or maybe I'm just sick. Do you think I'm sick?"

She was crying as well. "No, Scott."

"Then what?"

She choked on her words. "I guess we were just so much in love at the time. I know I was. You don't have to believe me, but it almost killed me to leave you that day." She sniffed and wiped her eyes, but it was no use, the tears continued to fall.

"I tried to imagine a life with you if you came out of that coma. The doctor said you had serious brain injuries and would never function normally even if you *did* live. I imagined you spending the rest of your life in a nursing home or in seclusion at your parents' house. I couldn't bear to watch you die, but worse than that, I couldn't stand the thought of you remaining in a vegetative state for the rest of your life.

"Not only that, I couldn't go back home, Scott. You know I couldn't have Kelly living under the same roof as my father. You wouldn't have wanted it either."

She hung her head and cried in silence while he stared at her in utter sadness. "You don't know what it's like to be labeled white trash, Scott. I lived with that for seventeen years, and I wasn't about to let Kelly go through it."

He crooked an index finger, placed it under her jaw, and raised her face so that she was looking into his eyes. "I never thought of you as trash, and you know it. All I'm trying to do is make life better for you and Kelly and Loretta," he said. "Why won't you let me help you?"

"Because," she sputtered. "Because you're doing it for all the wrong reasons."

He shook his head slightly. She wasn't making sense. "What are you talking about?"

"I'm not going to let you set me up like your father set up *his* women." When he looked at her strangely, she went on. "Surely you knew about his affairs."

"I would've had to be deaf, dumb, and blind not to," he responded tightly. "But what the hell does my father have to do with *us*? I'm not looking to make you my mistress, I'm just trying to provide for our daughter."

"Don't you see what you're doing? First you set Amy up in a nice house, then me."

Scott turned and slammed his fist against the front door, scaring Lucy so badly, she jumped. "Dammit, Lucy, are you just bound and determined to drive me insane in less than a week?"

She gazed at him silently, tears streaming down her

cheeks. "It's true, Scott. You're offering to do this only out of guilt."

"Why the hell should *I* feel guilty?" he bellowed, the sound echoing off the walls. "I was in a coma. Incapable of making life-changing decisions." He plunged his fingers into his hair, wondering if he'd ever understand her.

"Exactly. *I* was the one who left, *I* was the one who stayed away for fifteen years. You're off the hook, Scott. You don't have to fly puppies in from Jacksonville or buy us this big house."

Scott seemed to sag before her eyes. He walked over to the fireplace and sat down. He suddenly looked weary. And very sad. "Okay, Lucy," he said. "I don't even know why I bother."

Lucy's misery was like a lead weight in her heart as she took in his desolate features. It would have been so easy to accept his generous offer, but she had taken the easy way out once before and look what it had cost her. "I'll wait for you in the car," she said, slipping quietly out the door.

They made the drive back to Restful Valley in silence, the rain still coming down hard and making the day dreary. Lucy could see that Scott was upset with her, his square jaw was tense, his eyes hard and flat. He pulled into the parking space beside her car and waited for her to get out.

"Don't be angry with me," she said.

He didn't so much as look at her. "You're being selfish," he said. "I can afford to give my daughter a home where she won't have to share a bedroom with her mother or sleep under a leaky roof, but you're letting your damn stubborn pride stand in the way." He finally glanced her way, and she could see the hurt, the anger. "Tell me something," he said. "Why were you so agreeable to taking my father's money when you fight *me* every step of the way?"

She felt as though he'd slipped a knife between her ribs, the pain was so intense. Oh, how she regretted coming back to Shade Tree. She should have insisted her mother come to Atlanta. "I was desperate at the time. I've since learned to take care of myself."

He shook his head regretfully. "I think I liked you better when you were a bit more vulnerable, Lucy. When you needed me."

"You're right, I *did* need you desperately at one time. But you were torn from me, and I was forced to learn the hard way that I could count only on myself." Even as she said it, she realized her emotions were in serious conflict. While she still cared for him deeply, possibly loved him as much as she always had, she didn't want to be needy emotionally. She wanted to be with him, share with him what lovers shared, but she still wanted to hold on to that part of her she'd worked so hard to develop over the years. She wanted to know that she could make it on her own. Always.

Without another word, she opened her door and climbed out. The rain was cold on her face as she moved from his car to hers. It mingled with the warm tears on her cheeks.

The following Saturday afternoon Lucy drove to the hardware store and purchased several cans of beige paint and all the supplies she would need to go with it. She arrived home and unloaded her goodies as her mother watched, holding Champ in one arm. The dog was much like a baby, he had to be held all the time. He'd turned his nose up at the bed Loretta had made for him, choosing instead to sleep with Kelly.

"What are you going to paint?" Loretta said.

"The living room and hall."

"Well, it certainly needs it," she replied. "I don't remember the last time it was painted. I'll be glad to help, of course. If I can put this animal down for five minutes."

"Thank you. I'll take all the help I can get. Where's Kelly?"

"Scott came by to see if she wanted to go to a movie with Jeff and him. I didn't think you'd mind, so I said okay. They should be back around six."

Lucy nodded. "That's nice," she said, thankful Scott hadn't let their differences stand in the way of spending time with Kelly. "Would you help me drape the furniture with these drop cloths?"

"Let me see if I can coax Champ to sleep first." Loretta disappeared into Lucy and Kelly's bedroom. She stepped out a moment later, holding a finger to her lips.

"He curled up on Kelly's pillow and fell right to sleep," she said.

Lucy shook her head sadly. "You and Kelly are making mush out of that animal, you know that?"

"He's still a baby."

"He's a dog. You and Kelly have no business getting up in the middle of the night with him so he can have warm milk."

"Oh, but his tummy's so small, Lucy. He can't hold much, and the poor thing wakes up hungry in the middle of the night. What can we do?"

Kelly sighed heavily. One day she was going to walk into the kitchen and find Champ sitting in a high chair being spoon-fed at the kitchen table. "Mush," she said. "That's exactly what you two are making out of him."

Loretta sniffed. "You're one to talk. I've seen you mix baby cereal in his puppy food."

They exchanged their good-natured banter as they went about preparing the room. Taking great care not to wake Champ, Lucy slipped into her room and changed into old clothes, then went about spreading newspapers on the floor to catch paint spills. Finally, she opened the paint and stirred until she was sure it was mixed properly.

Some minutes later they were hard at work, Lucy using the roller and her mother edging with a paint-brush. Loretta had turned the radio on low so they could listen to music, and they chatted and hummed as they painted.

Loretta filled her in on the latest gossip at the plant, who was mad at whom, who had just gotten a promotion, and the latest romance. Lucy shared several funny stories about the nursing home, including the one where they'd had to pull a man out of one of the women's beds. "Thank goodness we know he's impotent," she said.

They took a brief coffee break, then went back to painting, not even aware of the time. "It's been nice having you and Kelly here," Loretta said. "I never invited friends over from the church when your father was alive because I didn't know what state he'd be in." She sighed. "Time passes so quickly, and then I look back and see how I wasted it and I just want to cry."

Lucy nodded. She could certainly relate to that.

"I tried to leave him once, you know," Loretta went on. "You were just a toddler at the time and wouldn't remember, but one day I just had had enough and bought us a bus ticket out of here."

Lucy looked surprised. "You never told me."

"I'd been saving money for months. Two or three dollars here, five dollars there. We ended up in Macon, Georgia, where I got a job in a coffee shop. I never had any real skills. I hired some girl to watch you while I worked, but it cost me almost everything I made to pay her. We almost starved to death. And she wasn't much of a baby-sitter. I'd come home and find the place dirty and you not taken care of, and I wanted to wring her neck.

"After about a month, Darnel showed up, claimed he was a changed man, and I agreed to give him another chance. Naturally, he went back to drinking, but after that experience in Macon, I was terrified of being on my own again." She was silent for a moment.

"I guess I have no right to say my life was a total waste though," she continued. "The Lord has His reasons for everything that happens to us. There's always a lesson to be learned."

"What could you have possibly learned by living with Darnel?" Lucy asked.

Loretta paused in her work, looking thoughtful. "Humility, maybe? If I'd have married a rich man, I might have placed too much emphasis on material wealth. I might have become so absorbed with this life that I wouldn't care about the next one." She chuckled, but her expression remained sad. "Living with Darnel taught me to look forward to the hereafter."

Lucy tried to think what she'd learned in fifteen years of living on her own. The only things that came to mind were her independence and her self-confidence. It pained her to think Scott preferred the *old* Lucy, who'd depended on him for everything, including her own happiness. She had no desire to be that person again. They might still be wildly attracted to each other, they might even feel sentimental at times and wish they could turn back the clock. But things could never be the same between them, nor would she want them to be.

The sound of a car out front reminded Lucy that it was almost six-thirty. A moment later Kelly stepped through the front door with Scott and Jeff on her heels, carrying pizzas.

"Be careful!" Loretta cautioned. "Wet paint everywhere."

"Oh, Grandma, it looks wonderful," Kelly said. The sound of her voice must have carried to the hall, because they suddenly heard Champ yapping from the bedroom.

"He's waking from his nap," Loretta said. "I knew if I didn't put him down, he'd be irritable later."

Kelly nodded. "I just hope he sleeps through the night for once. These night feedings are killing me." She hurried in the direction of her bedroom.

As Jeff was admiring the paint, Scott and Lucy exchanged glances. As usual, she was unable to read the expression on his face. He turned his gaze to Loretta.

"Why didn't you tell us you were having a paint party?" he said. "Jeff and I would have been glad to help. Right, Jeff?"

"Yeah, right, Dad." The boy rolled his eyes.

"Is that pizza I smell?" Loretta asked.

"As a matter of fact, it is. Why don't you take these into the kitchen?" Scott told his son, handing him the one he held. "I didn't know if you'd had dinner or not. I went by this place that was having a buy-one-get-one-free sale."

"You brought pizza into *this* house?" Lucy asked. "You know my mother isn't supposed to eat that sort of thing."

"I could just this once," Loretta pleaded.

"I ordered a vegetarian with half the usual amount of

cheese," Scott said. "Sorry, Loretta," he added with a wink.

Lucy came down off her stepladder. "Well, I suppose one or two pieces wouldn't hurt," she said.

Loretta beamed. "I hope you and Jeff will join us."

Once again Scott glanced in Lucy's direction. It was obvious he was waiting for her to invite them. "I don't want to barge in on you," he said.

"Don't be silly," Loretta replied, no doubt unaware of the tension between Scott and her daughter. "You and Jeff are family. You're always welcome here." She looked at Lucy. "Isn't that right?"

Lucy nodded, but she didn't quite meet Scott's gaze. "Of course."

Kelly returned holding the Yorkie in her arms, murmuring sweetly to him while he licked her face. "He missed me," she announced.

While the women scrubbed paint from their hands, Scott pulled a few extra chairs around the kitchen table so they could all fit. Loretta then passed out plates and napkins, and Lucy prepared glasses of iced tea.

"Kelly honey, please don't bring Champ to the table."

"But, Mom, he hates it when I put him down."

"He's going to have to learn some manners."

"My mom always lets Abby sit in her lap at the dinner table," Jeff said.

Lucy smiled, remembering how Abby had insisted on sitting on her lap that afternoon at Scott's. "I know, but everybody does things differently, and I'd rather Champ not get into the habit."

"Your mother's right," Scott said to Kelly. "You see how out of control Pepper is. If I had started training him early on, he wouldn't be such a nuisance now."

Kelly shrugged and put the puppy down, although he climbed and whimpered and made a big fuss.

Lucy started handing out slices of pizza, taking care to see that she and her mother got the vegetarian. "So what movie did ya'll see?" she asked, trying to ignore the dog scratching at Kelly's chair.

"That new Sylvester Stallone picture," Scott said, since Kelly and Jeff had their mouths full of pizza.

"Do you have Jeff every weekend?" Loretta asked.

Scott nodded. "He spends most weekends and summers at my place. I usually pick him up in the middle of the week, and we grab a bite to eat. It's a pretty informal arrangement."

"That's nice."

"By the way, I've been checking with roofers, and I think I've found just the guy for you."

"I hope he's cheap," Loretta mumbled.

"Yes, cheap just happens to be his middle name."

Lucy looked suspicious. "Who is he?"

"Me."

"You!" She almost shrieked the word.

Kelly and Jeff stopped chewing. The room went silent except for the puppy, who'd begun to whimper louder now.

"What's wrong with me?" Scott said, leaning back in his chair, regarding her quizzically.

"You don't know how to patch a roof."

"Who says I don't? I used to do all sorts of odd jobs during college."

Lucy tried not to smile. "Scott, you're not trying to tell me you *worked* your way through college. Not Aubrey Bufford's son."

He looked somewhat put off. "It's true my father put

me through college, Lucy. But all my spending money came from jobs I held during the summer."

The others continued to remain quiet, and Lucy suddenly realized it sounded as if she were picking on him. She felt her face grow warm. "I'm sorry, I didn't mean to imply—well, never mind. I just don't want you to get hurt falling off our roof, that's all."

They all went back to their pizza. Naturally, Lucy insisted Scott try a slice of the vegetarian.

"It's really quite good," Loretta said. "Until Lucy started hounding me about my diet—"

"I don't *hound* you, Mother."

"What I'm trying to say is, I was taught how to cook a certain way," Loretta said. "My mother used fat to season everything. It never occurred to me there was a healthier way to cook. And I'm proud to say, just since Lucy's been here I've lost eight pounds."

Lucy squealed with pleasure and hugged her mother. "I thought you looked thinner. Why didn't you say something?"

"I didn't want to make a fuss."

"Congratulations, Loretta," Scott said, offering his iced tea glass in a toast.

Kelly gave her grandmother the thumbs-up sign, then grabbed Champ and asked Jeff if he wanted to watch TV.

"Watch out for the wet paint," Lucy said.

"So what d'you say I come by tomorrow afternoon to get started on the roof?" Scott said. "The weatherman says it's going to be sunny."

In all honesty, Lucy thought they might be making a mistake. Not that she didn't appreciate his offer, of course, but she suspected the less time she spent with Scott the better. If he wanted to see Kelly, that was fine, but she knew it would be easier if she made herself scarce when he dropped by in the future. "It's supposed to be chilly," she said, trying to dissuade him.

He smiled, knowing she was trying her best to talk him out of it. "Yeah, it might plunge into the sixties," he joked. "I'll dig out my longjohns."

"Will you be able to find the shingles?"

"I can pick them up at the building supply store in town."

"That's awfully nice of you, Scott," Loretta said, getting up to clear the table. "Don't you think that's nice, Lucy?"

She met his gaze. "Yes, it's nice of him, although I'm certain he could find a more exciting way to spend a Sunday afternoon."

He could see the questions in her eyes. No doubt she thought he was crazy for offering to fix her roof when he would have gladly paid to have someone repair his own. He decided he must be a little bit crazy himself for doing it. But he knew she would never let him pay to have it done, and he couldn't stand the thought of them living under a leaky roof.

"I'm going to put on coffee, Scott," Loretta said. "Would you like some?"

He sensed Lucy was ready to see him go. It was nothing she'd said, of course, but he detected a difference in her. She was cool toward him.

"No thanks, Loretta. I thought I'd try to catch up on paperwork tonight while Jeff watched his television shows."

"Well, thanks again for the pizza," she said. "We'll have to have you and Jeff over for dinner sometime."

Lucy walked him to the living room, where the teenagers were staring at the TV screen. "Uh, Scott, about this roof business—" Lucy began.

"Don't make a big deal out of it, Luce. I'm only being neighborly."

"I don't want you to think I'm trying to take advantage."

He gave her a gentle smile. "You just don't want me to think you need me for anything. I can see right through you, Lucy Odum." He turned toward the teenagers. "Time to go, Jeff," he said.

The boy glanced over his shoulder. "Aw, Dad, why'd you wait till now? I'm right in the middle of my favorite show." Nevertheless, he stood and grabbed his nylon jacket.

"Kelly, don't you have something you'd like to say to your father?" Lucy asked, though it still sounded odd to say it.

"Oops!" The girl jumped up from the floor, and went over and kissed Scott on the cheek. "Thanks for the movie and pizza," she said. "Bye, Jeff."

Scott nodded toward Lucy but said nothing. She let out a long, audible breath as he and his son exited the front door and made their way to the car.

With an odd sense of disappointment, she watched them drive away a few minutes later, then picked up her paint roller and went back to work. If Loretta sensed tension between Scott and her daughter, she didn't say anything, just kept commenting on what a nice boy Jeff was. At midnight Loretta claimed she couldn't keep her eyes open any longer and went to bed.

Lucy put on another pot of coffee and kept going. Painting was a mindless task, she discovered. Her thoughts wandered, and she found herself thinking of Scott as the early morning hours wore on.

You just don't want me to think you need me for anything.
Tears moistened her eyes, but she refused to give in
to them. She was just tired and feeling sorry for herself.
At three A.M. she finished the job, then spent the next half
hour cleaning rollers and brushes. Kelly got up to feed
Champ, mumbling unintelligible words and yawning as
she waited for the puppy to wolf down his warm cereal
and relieve himself beside the back steps. Lucy scrubbed
up in the bathroom, slipped on a gown, and climbed into
bed.

Scott arrived the following afternoon in a battered
pickup truck that had gone to rust.

"Nice wheels," Kelly said, opening the front door to
greet him.

He grinned. "I borrowed it from my gardener," he
said. "Perhaps when you're sixteen I can buy you one just
like it. Is your mom around?"

"She and Grandma are still painting," Kelly said,
motioning him toward the hall. "I offered to help, but I
don't think they trust me with a paintbrush."

Scott found Lucy and Loretta sitting on the floor in
the hallway, slathering white paint on the baseboard.
"Sorry I'm late," he said. "Amy had car problems. I had
to find someone to tow it in. You know how some women
fall apart over silly things like a busted water hose."

"I suppose *some* women do," Loretta mumbled under
her breath.

"Anyway, I told her she could use my car until hers is
fixed."

"That was very nice of you," Lucy said, noting he
looked much like a roofer in old jeans and a sweatshirt.
"What are you supposed to drive in the meantime?"

"I'm covered. Well, I'm going to get started on the roof."

"Would you like a cup of coffee before you go?" Loretta asked.

"No, thanks." He left them, whistling as he went.

"That's too bad," Loretta said as soon as the front door closed behind him.

Lucy looked up from her work. "What's too bad?"

"The way he lets that woman lead him around by his short hairs. You'd think after all this time she'd have found another man to do her running. She's just playing on his guilt, if you ask me. No wonder the poor guy never remarried."

"Scott's a big boy," Lucy said. "I'm sure he can look after himself. Besides, it's none of our business."

They were both silent for a moment. Finally, Loretta laid down her paintbrush and sighed. "Aren't you even going to *try* to get him back?"

Lucy shot her a blank look. "Get him *back*?" she said dully. "I have no claim on Scott Bufford."

"You could if you wanted to. It's obvious as all get-out the boy still has feelings for you."

"Mother, he doesn't even like me anymore after what happened, and he *certainly* doesn't trust me."

"Which explains why he's up on the roof right now instead of sitting in front of some TV watching a football game and drinking a cold one like most men."

"He's doing it for Kelly."

"Bull."

Lucy shrugged. "Fine. Think what you like. I happen to know Scott."

"Are you going to tell me you don't feel anything for him?"

"Of course I feel something for him," Lucy said.

"He's Kelly's father. Naturally, I want the two of us to have an amicable relationship. But what we had before—" She paused. "That was fifteen years ago, and we were just kids."

"I don't think you're being honest with me *or* yourself," Loretta said. "If that's the case, then why haven't you married in all these years?"

"I didn't meet anyone I felt I could love."

"Because you were already in love with Scott."

"Could we just drop the subject?" Lucy asked. "I don't want Kelly overhearing any of this and getting the wrong idea."

"I'm just looking out for your happiness."

The phone rang. Kelly ran to answer it. "Mom, it's for you," she said. "Some woman."

Lucy put her brush down and pushed herself up from a squatting position so she could grab it. Amy Bufford spoke from the other end. "Lucy, is Scott over there by chance?"

"Yes, he is," Lucy said politely. "He's on the roof. Do you need to speak with him?"

"On the roof!" the other woman exclaimed. "What the heck is he doing there?"

"Making repairs. If you don't mind holding, I can go get him. Otherwise, I'll have him call you back."

"That's not necessary," Amy said. "Just ask him if he would be a dear and phone the garage for me. The guy over there called to tell me what I needed and how much it costs, and it was all Greek to me. Scott's so good at that sort of thing."

"I'll tell him," Lucy said. She hung up and hurried outside. She found Scott nailing tar paper in place. "Aren't you cold up there?" she asked, noting how red his face was.

"I'm okay, whatcha need?"

"Amy just called. She wants you to call the garage for her."

"I'll be down in a second."

Lucy continued to stand there. "It's none of my business, of course, but why can't *she* talk to the mechanic?"

"Amy doesn't understand cars, and she's afraid the guy will sell her something she doesn't need. I'm sure you've heard how auto repair shops sometimes rip women off."

"I suppose the secret to avoiding that is to find a mechanic you trust."

He climbed down from the roof, using the ladder from his truck. "You got a problem with me helping Amy?" he asked curiously.

"No, of course not. But if you keep running to her rescue, she won't learn how to handle these things herself. What's she going to do should her car break down while she's out of town?"

"Probably have the mechanic call me long distance to explain the problem."

Lucy shrugged as she started for the house. "Well, it's always nice to have someone take care of that sort of thing for you, but I like knowing I can do for myself."

"I guess that means you're pretty self-sufficient."

"Guess so," she replied, wondering if he'd meant it as a compliment or criticism.

They paused at the door as Scott reached for the knob first. "I feel sorry for you, Lucy. That you can go through life not needing anyone. I suppose that's why it was so easy for you to walk out on everybody who loved you fifteen years ago."

SEVEN

He was uncomfortably close. The wind had tossed his dark hair about; several locks fell casually on his forehead. "That's not fair," she blurted out.

"You're right. I'm beating a dead horse, aren't I? Some people aren't capable of change, and I think you might be one of them."

She thought he looked sad. "What's wrong with me the way I am, Scott?" She really wanted to know why he insisted on finding fault with her.

He gazed at her for a moment. "Oh, Lucy," he said with a sigh. "Don't you ever wish we could go back—"

"No!" she said, almost shouting the word. "I have no desire to return to the past. You forget, Scott, I didn't have it as good as you did. I had Darnel to deal with. While your mother was taking you to Savannah and Charleston for school clothes, I was wearing secondhand clothes and scraping plates at school in order to receive free lunches."

He looked confused. "How could you not have had

lunch money, when your mother worked every day of her life?"

"Because my father spent it on booze, Scott. After a while I just stopped eating lunch at school because I couldn't bear the thought of the other kids laughing at me behind my back. Now, why in hell would I want to take a trip back to the old days?"

"I'm sorry, Lucy. I didn't mean it literally. I just meant—" He paused and looked at his shoes. "I don't know what I meant. I guess I never knew how bad you really had it. You kept a lot from me."

Which was true. She hadn't wanted him to feel sorry for her. "Well, it's all in the past now," she said.

"We were going to be married, Lucy. As my wife, you would never have wanted for anything."

"Must we go through that again?"

"If only you'd hung around a little longer."

She gazed at him for a long while. Talking to him was like talking to a brick wall, and she was tired of it, tired of protecting him when all it did was create more hard feelings between them. "Come with me." She reached for his hand. It shook her that after all these years their hands seemed to fit together so perfectly.

Scott looked wary as she led him around the house to the backyard. "Where are you taking me?"

"I have something to show you."

He followed her to the garage, and they entered through a door at the rear. Inside, it was dark and musty. Lucy released his hand, groped for the light switch, and flipped it on.

Scott wished she hadn't let go of his hand. "What's all this?" he said, nodding toward the boxes and furniture.

"Everything I own," she said. She went straight for

the stack of boxes, reading from the outside what she'd listed as the contents.

"Lucy, what are you doing?" Scott said as she continued her search.

"Hold your britches on," she said. "Ah-ha! Here it is." She pulled a box from the stack and carried it over, then managed to rip off the packing tape. She fumbled inside and pulled out a white Bible. After flipping through several pages, she found what she wanted and handed it to Scott.

"What is it?" he said.

"Your obituary."

"My *what*?" The look he gave her was incredulous.

"Read it."

Scott carried the article closer to the light and read. "My Lord, where did you get this?"

She hesitated. "Your father sent it to me."

His eyes were guarded when he looked up. "I hope you're not playing games with me."

"I'm telling you the truth, Scott. Whether you choose to believe me is entirely up to you."

He read it again, noting that someone had gone to a great deal of trouble to make it look authentic. He was not surprised, especially now that he knew his father had lied to him about the baby being born dead. Scott sat down. Only then did he realize he was trembling from head to foot. "Why didn't you show me this before?"

"I didn't want to hurt you worse than you'd already been hurt." Lucy paused. "I had no desire to leave you that day in the hospital, Scott. I didn't want to have to watch you die, but if you were going to, I wanted to hold your hand until your last breath. Your father didn't want me there. He wanted you all to himself.

"I stood up to him at first. I told him I had no intention of leaving. Then"—she paused again—"he threatened to take Kelly away from me."

Scott muttered a curse.

"I had every confidence he would follow through. He considered me trash. Not once did he bother to go down to the hospital nursery and look at our baby, because he assumed she wasn't yours. He thought I was after the money.

"I was seventeen years old, Scott. Unmarried and unemployed with no place to go. It was either give up my baby or leave town. He made the decision easier by offering to pay for my education. I took it because I wanted to make something of myself. I didn't want Kelly to grow up under Darnel's roof."

Scott continued to stare at his obituary. "He obviously had this printed at the plant."

"I didn't know there was a print shop," Lucy said, "and it never occurred to me that he would—"

"Stoop so low?" Scott said.

Those were the words she would have used had they not been discussing his father. "I don't have proof of everything I'm telling you," she said. "Just that," she added, nodding toward the obituary he still held.

He crumpled it up and tossed it aside, his shock quickly yielding to fury. How could he have been so blind? Why had he simply accepted everything his father had told him? It explained so many things: why he'd been moved from the hospital so quickly, the reason he hadn't heard from friends. His father had literally kept him prisoner with only Amy to care for him, and he'd been so depressed over losing Lucy and the baby that he'd welcomed the solitude.

"You don't need proof, Lucy," he said at last. "I believe every word you're saying. I'm sorry you had to go through that, and I'm sorry for the way I've treated you since you returned." He shook his head. "I'm sorry as hell, Lucy." He said the words softly, but there was no denying the cold contempt in his voice. His dark eyes glittered.

Apprehension gnawed at Lucy as she watched him deal with his anger. "I don't blame you, Scott," she said. "You had no way of knowing."

He suddenly looked sad. "I knew my father was shrewd and conniving. I had no idea he was so . . ." He tried to think of the right word.

She put a finger to his lips. "Don't say it, Scott. Don't say anything you might regret later. Aubrey loved you very much, so much that he was willing to do anything to get me out of your life."

"How can you defend him?"

"I'm not defending him, but I know what it's like to love your child so much, you'll do just about anything to protect him or her. I feel that way about Kelly." She paused. "At the same time, there's a part of me that hopes Aubrey lived to regret his actions."

"I think he probably did," Scott said. "When he saw how unhappy and miserable I was without you. I had absolutely no desire to live once he'd told me you were gone.

"He also saw what it was like for me marrying a woman I didn't love. He knew I wasn't happy. Once, he even told me to take a mistress."

"Did you?"

"Of course not. I figured I'd cheated Amy enough. But she wasn't stupid. Why do you think she divorced me? She was as much a victim as I was."

They were both quiet for a moment. Scott stepped closer. He took her hands in his. "Where does this leave us, Lucy? Do you think we have a chance after all these years?" His voice was thick and unsteady.

He looked so sincere, she felt her heart turn over in her chest. "I don't know. So much has happened. We've changed. I'm not the person I was."

"I never stopped loving you," he said. "I may have hated you at times, but the love was always there."

She felt her eyes mist over as her heart swelled with emotions she had thought long since dead. "I can't believe we've wasted fifteen years."

"We can make up for it now, Luce," he said, hope in his voice. "We're still young, we have the rest of our lives. We can start over fresh, as though none of this ever happened."

"Do you think that's really possible?"

He nodded and pulled her into his arms, then tilted her head back so she was forced to look at him. He felt his blood rushing through his veins like an awakened river that had been stagnant only moments before. "Would you go to dinner with me tonight? Just the two of us. I know a candlelit place in the next town that's real romantic. We've got a lot of catching up to do."

She nodded. The thought of spending time alone with Scott was unbelievably appealing.

"I'll pick you up at seven. That'll give me time to patch some of the roof before I have to run home and shower." He kissed her lightly on the lips, then slid his arms around her waist and kissed her again, this time slipping his tongue inside her mouth. Lucy felt her body grow hot. They didn't even hear the garage door open or the embarrassed cough that followed.

"Oh, pardon me."

Loretta was standing there—embarrassed, yet jubilant. They stepped apart quickly.

"What is it?" Lucy said.

Loretta looked at Scott. "Amy's on the phone. She wants to know if you called the mechanic. Do you want me to tell her you'll call her back?"

Scott shook his head. "No, I'll take the call," he said. He squeezed Lucy's hand briefly, then hurried out of the garage, leaving her to wonder how she would ever reclaim her place in his life when he felt so obligated to another woman.

Lucy was already dressed in her nicest outfit when Scott called at six-thirty with a change of plans.

"I don't know what I was thinking when I offered to take you to that restaurant," he said. "I'm still driving my gardener's pickup truck. Do you mind if we go casual tonight instead?"

"That's fine," Lucy said. She hurried in to change, taking care not to wrinkle the dress she'd ironed so carefully. It didn't occur to her until after she'd stepped into slacks and pulled on a sweater that they could have used her car. Of course, it didn't matter in the least where they had dinner as long as they were together.

Loretta came out of her bedroom and did a double-take. She'd been smiling and humming gospel tunes under her breath since she'd caught them kissing in the garage. Now she looked worried. "Why'd you change clothes?" she asked. "Are you and Scott not going out after all?"

"He just realized he was driving an old pickup truck and decided we should slum it tonight instead of going fancy."

"Amy still has his car, right? It figures."

"She can't help the fact that her car's in the shop," Lucy said.

"You're right. But why does she always have to run to Scott when there's a problem?"

Lucy was beginning to wonder the same thing, then reminded herself Amy was Jeff's mother and would remain a part of Scott's life no matter what. She would simply have to accept it. Perhaps in time, Amy would back off.

Scott arrived almost twenty minutes late, just as Loretta and Kelly were sitting down to a meal of baked chicken, steamed vegetables, and a salad with low-fat dressing. Feeling a bit put out due to his tardiness, Lucy said good-bye to her mother and daughter and followed him out to the truck.

"I should have suggested we use my car," she said as he helped her in on the passenger side. The seats were old and cracked and smelled of dirt and grass clippings.

"And miss having your old friends see you in this dinosaur?" he said.

She chuckled and waited for him to join her in the front seat. He looked sexy in jeans, a rugby shirt, and a lightweight jacket, but she doubted there was anything he wouldn't look good in.

"Sorry I'm late," Scott said. "I had to drop Jeff off first, and Amy insisted I look at his report card. The kid is really slipping in algebra, and his mother thinks it's time we hire a tutor and take some of his privileges away. I would have called, but as you can see, I haven't had time to install a cellular phone."

"So Jeff's grounded, huh?"

"Looks that way."

"Do you and Amy always agree on how he should be disciplined?"

He nodded. "Always. Amy knows more about kids than I could ever hope to learn. She's taken a number of child psychology courses for her job. Sadly enough, many of her patients are children who've been in some sort of accident."

Lucy was thankful now that she hadn't been hired at the hospital. She couldn't imagine having to work in the same facility as Scott's ex-wife. It was taxing enough just hearing how perfect she was.

They chatted easily as Scott drove, reminiscing about bygone days. Scott gave her a rundown on their old friends, who'd married whom, who'd gone to college and relocated, and who was still living in Shade Tree. They pulled into the parking lot of a rather shabby-looking restaurant called Barefoot Bubba's Barbecue.

"Remember this place?" Scott said, turning to her.

Lucy shook her head in amazement. They'd gone there as kids and had eaten their fill of barbecue and onion rings. "I can't believe it's still standing. Lord, it was falling apart fifteen years ago."

He chuckled. "It still is. Every time a board falls loose, Bubba just nails it back up." His eyes turned soft. "I guess the only thing that's gotten better-looking in all that time is you."

She looked at him. The smile on her face faded, and her own look turned tender. "What a sweet thing to say."

Scott slipped his arm along the back of the seat and curled his hand around her neck. "Come here."

She scooted closer. They gazed at each other. Suddenly, she glanced away, feeling self-conscious.

He noted the troubled look on her face. "What is it, Lucy?"

She shrugged. "I guess I'm out of practice. Contrary to what my pride led you to believe, I haven't had a whole lot of experience where the opposite sex is concerned."

"I suppose it would be selfish of me to say that I'm relieved. Still, I hate the thought of you being lonely all those years."

"I wasn't all that lonely. I had Kelly and several close friends. I dated, but never got serious with anyone. That seemed to be enough at the time."

"What about now?" he asked gently. "Do you think you might be ready for a relationship? With me, I mean?"

Lucy felt her heart swell with emotion as she gazed once again into his eyes. He was laying his feelings on the line, opening his heart to her, and she had no choice but to respond in honesty. Even if it meant taking a risk, of becoming vulnerable. "I never stopped loving you, Scott," she said. "Never stopped wanting you."

He took a deep breath and leaned close. Their foreheads touched. "Stop right there, Lucy Odum," he said, giving her a look of warning. "Or I'm going to turn this truck around and take you home with me without feeding you."

She chuckled, but her insides warmed at the thought of spending time alone with him. She noted the sudden hunger in his eyes, but suspected he wasn't exactly craving barbecue at the moment. "If you keep looking at me like that, ol' Bubba's likely to kick us out."

He released her with a heavy sigh.

They went inside and slid into a booth. Nothing had changed, not even the mouth-watering smells. A freckle-faced waitress in a short denim skirt and hot-pink T-shirt greeted them. They ordered root beers in tall, frosty mugs and an appetizer of onion rings.

"I feel so guilty eating this," Lucy said once the platter of onion rings had been delivered and they'd ordered ribs for their main course. "All I've done is preach healthy eating to my mother since I've been back."

"I'll tell Loretta you ate radishes and celery sticks," Scott said.

"She's like a bloodhound. She'll smell fried food on my clothes."

He chuckled. "We can stop by my place. I'll throw your clothes in the washer while you shower. I should have a spare toothbrush somewhere."

They both laughed. He toasted her with his mug. "Welcome back, Luce," he said.

She suddenly felt very emotional. "I'm glad to be back."

Their ribs arrived, messy with barbecue sauce, and they went through a stack of napkins as they ate and continued to go on about old times. "What ever happened to Thelma Potter?" Lucy asked, remembering her old high school chum.

"She married and moved to Tampa. She comes once or twice a year, mostly holidays, to visit her family. If you like, I can probably find her address for you."

"Maybe once I've settled in," Lucy said. She still felt like a stranger in town. She licked barbecue sauce off her fingers, and Scott watched her pink tongue, transfixed.

"Oh, man, I wish you wouldn't do that," he said thickly.

"Scott!" She felt a blush creep to her cheeks. She leaned closer. "You've got a dirty mind, Mr. Bufford." Still, it was fun to play. She picked up another rib and made a production of licking the sauce off it, sliding her tongue the length of it.

Scott shifted in his seat. He could feel himself becoming aroused just watching her. He cleared his throat and tried to remember what they'd been talking about. "Remember Shelly Framer?" he said, trying not to let his thoughts run in another direction. "The girl who wore all that eye makeup and bleached her hair?"

Lucy nodded. "How can I forget? She had quite a reputation with the football team. Whatever happened to her?"

"She married a preacher."

"No!"

"They live in Bramley, about sixty miles from here. Last I heard they had six kids."

"Who would have believed it?" Once again she began licking sauce off her fingers.

Scott watched her slide her index finger almost completely into her mouth and pull it out slowly. It was shiny and slippery. He almost groaned. Then, from the corner of his eye, he noted the two men at the next table were watching her as well. "Lucy?"

"Yes?"

"Stop that."

She gazed back innocently. "I beg your pardon?"

"You know what I'm talking about. If you keep that up, I will be in no condition to walk out of this restaurant."

They finished their ribs and turned down the waitress's offer of Key lime pie, deciding on coffee instead. "It's still early," Scott said after he'd paid their check. "You feel like taking in a movie?"

She shook her head. "I'd rather just talk. Is there somewhere we—"

"We could go to my place," he said, although he knew once he got her there, talking would be the last thing on his mind. "It's less than ten minutes from here."

She chuckled. "It's a small town, Scott. You can get to *anywhere* in less than ten minutes."

They left the restaurant a few minutes later and climbed into the battered truck. Once they were on their way, Lucy turned to him. "I keep forgetting to ask you how Mike is."

Scott smiled. "Oh, my little brother is quite busy these days. He and his wife have three children now; the youngest is just a few months old."

"Oh, goodness!"

"I've sort of taken over most of the traveling until my new nephew settles in."

"Do you travel often?" she asked.

He grinned. "Well, until you showed up I tried to visit a different plant every week, at least for a couple of days. My father bought a plane some years back, so it makes it a lot easier getting around."

"Scott, I don't expect you to change your work schedule just because I'm back."

He glanced at her. "Why not?"

The question surprised her. "Because it's your job."

"I've devoted the past ten years of my life to those plants," he said. "I don't expect business will go down the tubes if I slack off a bit. You know, I can't remember when I last had a vacation. Now that you're back, maybe it'll give me a reason to take one. With a plane at our disposal, we could go anywhere we like."

She laughed. "Have you forgotten I just started a new job?" she asked. "I have to be there at least six months before I get a week's vacation."

"Minor details," Scott said. "If they know you're going with me, they'll be only too happy to let you have the time off."

"What's that supposed to mean?" she asked, although she knew *exactly* what he'd meant.

He didn't hesitate. "I'm sure you're aware the Bufords have invested heavily in Restful Valley, Lucy, and that I'm on the board of directors. Who do you think is putting up most of the money for the future retirement center?"

"And because of that, you think I should receive special treatment?" she asked.

He glanced at her. "Don't you?"

She looked away. "I'm sort of used to earning rewards the old-fashioned way," she said. "By working for them." She was thoughtful for a moment. "Who approved my application, Scott?"

"I did. I figured it was the least I could do after I'd raised such a stink. It was just a formality, of course. Alice had already made it clear she wanted you for the job."

"And who set my salary?"

"Why do you ask?"

"During my interview, Alice stated she couldn't meet my previous salary. Then, when she formally offered me the job, she met it to the penny. Did you have anything to do with that?"

He hedged. "I may have mentioned the fact that we should be prepared to pay more for someone with your experience. It's not as if you'd just graduated from nursing school. You had an impressive number of years behind you."

Lucy realized their situation was awkward. "Look, Scott, I really appreciate your support, but I think it would be best in the future if someone else from the board handled decisions regarding my employment. If my coworkers suspected I was getting preferential treatment because of our relationship—well, that might cause hard feelings."

"You're making a big deal out of this, Lucy. I would never have approved the hiring if you hadn't been perfect for the job." He paused. "But if it'll make you feel better, I'll go along with your request."

"Thank you." He nodded, but she could see he was deep in thought. "What is it?" she said.

He shrugged. "I want you to like your job and all, but I guess I want to take priority in your life."

"You do take priority, Scott. But I still have to earn a living and see that Kelly gets her share of attention."

He turned into his driveway a moment later and cut the engine. Finally, he turned in the seat and faced her. "You're probably going to think I'm selfish for saying this, but I have no intention of sharing you with a lot of people right now. I realize your job is important, but jobs come and go. I also realize we have a daughter, but she'll grow up one day and move away, and there'll still be us. I want to come first in your life, Luce, because I plan to put you first in mine. I refuse to settle for anything less."

Lucy felt unnerved by his intense gaze. "I don't know what to say," she answered honestly. "Aren't you afraid we're moving kind of fast on this?"

He shook his head. "From the moment I laid eyes on you, I knew I wanted you back. Despite the rage and hurt and everything else that happened in my life, that one thing remained constant."

"I have a question," she said softly. "What would you have done if I'd come back to Shade Tree while you were still married to Amy?"

He didn't hesitate. "Well, once I discovered the real

reason you'd left, I would've had no choice but to ask Amy for a divorce. She married me knowing I still had feelings for you."

"Do you think she had any knowledge of what your father did?"

He shook his head. "She wouldn't have stooped to trickery. Besides, my father wasn't exactly overjoyed at the prospect of us marrying. He wanted me to marry into a wealthy family. He just went along with it because—"

"Because marrying Amy was a step above marrying into white trash," she said.

Scott took her hand. "I don't hold you responsible for your father's mistakes," he said. "I hope you won't begrudge me for my father's sins."

"I'm just glad we've been given a second chance," she replied.

Scott raised her hand to his lips and kissed it. "Me too." Still holding it, he opened his door, climbed out, and helped her out as well. From out of nowhere, Pepper rushed to greet them.

"Down, Pepper!" he ordered. The dog saw the open door to the truck and jumped in. Lucy laughed as Scott tried to convince him to come out. Finally, he grabbed Pepper's front legs and dragged him across the seat. Once out, Pepper pounced on Lucy. "I have no control over that animal," Scott said. "Just make a run for it." They raced to the front door, pausing while Scott unlocked it. Laughing almost hysterically, Lucy ducked behind Scott in an attempt to escape Pepper's affections.

"This is embarrassing," he said, almost shoving Lucy into the house as he tried to keep the animal from following. "I can't have anybody over without my dog slobbering all over them."

"He'll grow out of it," she said, still laughing.

"Here, let me take your coat."

She shrugged out of her jacket and handed it to him. He hung it up in a front closet with his own. "You want something to drink?" he said. "More coffee?"

"No, heavens, if I drink another cup, I'll never get to sleep tonight."

"How about a glass of white wine, then?"

She sensed he was as anxious as she. "Just water, if you don't mind."

"Have a seat." He motioned to the sofa. "Kick your shoes off if it'll make you more comfortable."

She slipped out of her sneakers and sunk into the plump sofa. She studied the photographs before her, mostly of Jeff in various stages of his life: Jeff as a youngster with missing front teeth, Jeff and Scott standing beside a boat, holding up several large fish, Jeff waterskiing. A larger picture showed Amy and Scott at Jeff's christening. Amy, in a light colored suit, was the epitome of wife and motherhood; Scott the proud father. Lucy tried to remember what she'd been doing during that time. Probably in her second year of nursing school.

Suddenly, she felt depressed. Fifteen years. It sounded like a lifetime. Actually, it *was* a lifetime. At seventeen, she'd been little more than a kid with a baby to raise. She'd been frightened and insecure with no clue as to what she wanted to do with her life. Luckily, she'd been influenced by a young nurse who'd cared for her shortly after the accident. Even in her battered state, she'd questioned the girl about educational requirements and had decided nursing might not be such a bad way to make a living. Now she was a grown woman, and her baby was a young girl who would be making career decisions of her own before long. Yes, fifteen years *was* a lifetime when you studied it up close.

Scott walked into the room and noted the pensive, almost sad look on her face. "What's wrong?" he asked.

"Huh?" Lucy glanced up. "Oh, nothing, I was just thinking."

He set a glass of ice water on the coffee table and took a seat next to her. "What is it, Luce?"

"Kelly and I should be in that picture beside you."

He glanced at the picture of him and Amy and Jeff and wished he'd thought to put it away. But how *could* he put it away? Amy was Jeff's mother. What would the boy think when he noticed it missing?

"You're right, Lucy," Scott said at last. "It should have been you, me, and Kelly. But that's not the way it happened. We can either accept it and make the best of it, or spend the rest of our lives bemoaning the years we lost."

"You knew I was out there somewhere. Why didn't you come after me, Scott?" She looked up at him, puzzled and hurt.

He sighed and clasped his hands together. "In the beginning, I was too angry. I honestly believed you left because you feared I might be severely handicapped. That made me even more determined to walk and live normally again. As time progressed, my pride got in the way. I told myself I didn't need you, convinced myself I was better off without you. Then—" He paused, not knowing how to put it.

"You fell in love with Amy?"

He shook his head. "I never loved her. At least not the way a man *should* love his wife." He looked at her through emotion-packed eyes. "Not the way I loved you."

"But you married her anyway?"

"Yes. And I don't regret it for a minute, because of Jeff."

Lucy was quiet for a moment. "I don't know where I fit in, Scott."

He pulled her close. "Where do you fit in?" he asked solemnly. "In my heart, where you've always been."

Lucy sighed. She felt as though her own heart were near bursting. A lump filled her throat.

His steady gaze bore into hers, searching her eyes before dropping to her shoulders and finally her breasts. A vaguely sensuous light passed between them. "I want to make love to you, Luce," he said. "Not like when we were kids. I want to make love to you as a man."

Lucy felt like a breathless seventeen-year-old again. She studied the handsome face, and she felt a curious tug inside. Her belly warmed while other parts of her body tensed. She picked up her glass, took a sip. Scott had dropped a lemon wedge inside. Wasn't it just like him to go to so much trouble for her? She watched him over the rim of her glass, saw the tender longing in his eyes. What would it be like after all these years? She couldn't deny the spark of excitement she felt at the prospect of being held in his arms again.

"Yes," she said.

He rewarded her with a smile that was made even more dazzling by the look in his eyes. He stood and offered his hand, then led her slowly toward the bedroom.

"Scott?"

He paused in the doorway and looked at her. He noted the tension in her face and wished she could just relax. "Yes?"

"I'm not taking birth control pills or anything like that."

He nodded, led her farther into the room, and released her hand. "I'll be right back."

Lucy watched him make his way into the bathroom, heard him open the medicine cabinet. He stepped out, leaving the light on and cracking the door so he would be able to see what he was doing. Then he realized Lucy might not feel comfortable.

"You want me to cut the light?"

"No, it's fine."

He nodded and dropped a small foil packet onto the night table before taking her in his arms. He held her close, taking in the smell of her perfume, the feel of her body against his. "Oh, Lucy," he said, his breath at her ear. "I can't believe I finally have you in my arms again. It's been—" His voice broke with huskiness. "It's been so long."

Lucy slipped her arms around his waist and locked her fingers together. He was so warm and virile, so full of life. "I know," she whispered.

He kissed her deeply, lovingly, tasting the inside of her mouth with an impatient tongue. A hot ache grew low in his belly, and he felt himself become hard. He took her hand and guided it to that part of his body. A shiver ran through him as she pressed her open palm against him.

"Undress me," he ordered.

Lucy reached for the buttons on his shirt and undid them with trembling fingers. She marveled at his solid, hair-rough chest and slid her fingers through the crisp curls. She could feel his muscles tighten beneath her fingertips. Playfully, she nipped his nipples with her teeth, and his broad shoulders heaved with the next breath he drew.

"Oh, Lord," he said on a shaky sigh, then chuckled at his own sad state of arousal. He felt her unbuckle his belt, heard his zipper whisper open. As bad as he wanted to feel her hands on him, he knew he'd never last if he gave her full reign over his body. "Enough," he said, stilling her hands and willing himself to take control.

Lucy looked surprised. "You don't like it?"

He captured her face between his hands and kissed her. "I like it too much, babe. We need to move slowly, okay?"

The last thing she wanted to do was stop touching him, but when she opened her mouth to protest, he covered it with his own and kissed her until she was too dizzy to object. She felt him lift her sweater. He stopped kissing her long enough to pull it over her head. Next, he unfastened her bra, then pulled back so he could gaze down at her. The look in his eyes almost took her breath away.

Scott studied her perfect breasts. They were fuller than he remembered, no doubt a result of her matured body. At seventeen she'd been self-conscious about them, claiming they were too small. "Did you nurse Kelly?" he asked softly.

Lucy nodded. "Yes."

He stroked them lightly, watching in fascination as her nipples grew hard. "I would like to have been there for that."

Only then did Lucy realize how selfish she'd been. She had spent so much time feeling crummy for having been denied the past fifteen years with him that she hadn't once considered what Scott had missed out on.

He removed the rest of her clothes in haste, impatient to gaze at her nakedness. She had filled out, ripened. Where she'd once been on the skinny side, she now had womanly curves. He suspected he could lose himself with her, forget the rest of the world existed.

"You're beautiful," he said.

Suddenly, he lifted her high in his arms. He carried her to the bed and laid her down. She swept the covers aside as he kicked off his shoes and stepped out of his jeans and underwear. Lucy smiled. "My, my, you're all grown up, Mr. Bufford."

He joined her on the bed and gathered her in his arms. He kissed her deeply, greedily, pulling away when their need for oxygen became great. Lucy pressed her face against his chest, inhaled his clean, masculine scent as he stroked her back and hips. He touched her, cupping her breasts, sliding his fingers down her flat belly, marveling at her satiny skin. He touched her with tantalizing possessiveness, his skills sharpened by his desire to please. He dipped his fingers between her thighs, and to his immense pleasure, found her wet.

His mouth followed the path his hands had made; sucking at her breasts and biting her nipples lightly with his teeth until she moaned and plunged her fingers into his thick hair. He ran his tongue down her stomach, encircled her navel, and followed her musky scent. He tasted her for the first time.

Lucy stiffened the minute she felt Scott's tongue make intimate contact with her body. She clutched the bedcovers with her hands as he touched and sampled her body with his lips, drawing sighs from her, making her tingle and tremble. This was not the seventeen-year-old boy who'd made love to her in his car or on blankets spread on the grass. The harsh, uneven sound of her breathing told her he was a man who knew his way around women. She barely had time to register the brief pain of that thought because of the urgency that drove her. She arched against him, moaning aloud with erotic pleasure, then soared to heights of passion that left her quivering and chanting his name as if it were a well-loved song.

Still tasting Lucy on his lips, Scott fumbled with the condom, swept her legs apart, and entered her. He cursed under his breath as she sheathed him tightly and drove away all rational thought. His mind became fragmented, only his senses remained, the taste and smell and feel of Lucy beneath him. He buried himself deep inside, and suddenly he knew why kings abandoned their thrones for the love of a woman.

His orgasm was powerful; he vibrated with liquid fire. Their bodies fused, souls embraced. And when the fire inside him became quiet again, he felt as though he'd been reborn.

Time passed. The perspiration on their bodies began to dry. Holding Lucy tight against him, Scott suddenly realized she was crying. "Are you okay?"

Lucy couldn't have formed a coherent response if her life had depended on it. She turned her face and nuzzled against Scott's chest.

Scott raised himself up on one elbow and gazed down at her. The sight of her tears made him afraid. "What's wrong, babe? Why are you crying?"

She looked up at him, thinking he'd never been more handsome or desirable. She sniffed. "I just—" Another sniff and a small hiccup. "I just love you so much."

Scott scratched his head as confusion battled relief. "So why are you crying?"

"I—I just can't keep it in. My heart feels like it's going to explode because I'm so happy."

He chuckled and pulled her on top of him. "I love you too, Lucy Odum. And if you ever leave me again, I'm going to wring your neck with my bare hands."

EIGHT

The next few weeks passed in a whirlwind as Scott and Lucy spent almost every free moment together. They included the kids and Loretta when they could, of course. There were cookouts and swimming at Scott's, paint parties at Loretta's, not to mention bowling and movies and frequent dinners at Barefoot Bubba's Barbecue. When they could, Lucy and her mother visited garage sales and antique stores, looking for good buys on used furniture. Lucy was determined to get the house in the best shape possible.

For her mother's birthday, Lucy purchased an old claw-foot table of solid oak with four matching chairs. Someone had painted it yellow years before, then stuck it in a barn with more old stuff. Lucy got it for a fraction of the cost she would have paid in a store. She and Scott stripped the table and chairs and stained them. Loretta, who'd been forbidden to come close to the garage since the project began there, was beside herself with joy the day she came home from work and found the dining room set in her kitchen.

The following week Scott had an entire living room suite delivered to the house, claiming they were redecorating the reception area in one of his plants and no longer needed the furniture. Lucy couldn't believe what good condition it was in. Her mother's little house was finally beginning to look nice.

One afternoon, as Lucy was preparing to leave for the day, Scott walked into Restful Valley with Kelly. Lucy looked surprised. "What's going on?"

He smiled and put his arm around his daughter. "What do you say we take my mother out for an early dinner?" he suggested. "I think it's time she met her granddaughter."

The three of them led a rather confused-looking Naomi into the Shade Tree Yacht Club less than an hour later. Lucy was glad Kelly had changed into proper attire before showing up with Scott; she wore her nicest dress. Scott had introduced her as Lucy's daughter, obviously waiting until the right moment to tell Naomi the truth.

Inside the plush dining room he ordered a bottle of champagne, then remembered his mother was on different medications and asked Lucy if she would be able to have a glass. Lucy assured him a small glass wouldn't hurt.

"Champagne?" Naomi said, looking at the three suspiciously. "Would someone please tell me what's going on?"

While the waiter hurried away to get the champagne, Scott took his mother's hand in his. "Mom, do you know who Lucy really is?" he asked gently.

"I didn't at first," she replied. "Now I do. She's the girl your father tried so desperately to keep you away from." She looked sad as she said it.

"He succeeded for fifteen years," Scott said.

Naomi looked at Lucy. "I'm sorry. I tried to convince Aubrey more than once to back off where you and Scott were concerned because I was afraid he'd alienate our son. But he didn't listen to me." She paused. "My husband was accustomed to having his own way." She glanced at Kelly, then back at Lucy. "So you married after you left Shade Tree?"

"I've never been married," Lucy replied.

Naomi looked surprised. "Then, who—" Her cheeks flushed red. "Sorry, it's none of my business."

"Mom, Kelly is *my* daughter," Scott said gently. "*Your* granddaughter."

The woman gasped. "But how can that be? I was told the baby was stillborn."

"I'm afraid we were misled," he said gently.

Naomi gazed at Kelly for a moment, and her eyes filled with tears. "Oh, my. One only has to look at her to see the resemblance." Naomi reached for her purse, fumbled in it for a tissue, and dabbed her eyes. She regarded Lucy. "Why did you leave?" she asked. "Why did you take my granddaughter from me?"

Scott took his mother's hand in his. "It wasn't Lucy's fault, Mom. Father threatened to have Kelly taken away from her if she didn't leave town."

Naomi looked shocked. She shook her head. "Aubrey wouldn't go that far."

"He did it," Scott replied tersely. "He even convinced Lucy I'd died."

Naomi started to cry, and Lucy was glad they were the only customers in the restaurant. She reached for the woman's hand and squeezed it. "Please don't cry, Mrs. Bufford," she said. "This should be a happy time for us."

"I should have known," Naomi said. "If Aubrey was able to lie to me about the other women in his life, what was to stop him from lying about everything else?" She regarded Scott tearfully. "Folks said I was blind to your father's affairs. Ha! I knew what was going on, it's not like your father was discreet by any means. I *chose* to ignore the rumors and the evidence because I suspected your father would simply tell me to leave if I didn't like it. I didn't want to give up the prestige of being Mrs. Aubrey Bufford."

"That's in the past now, Mom," Scott said.

"I should have stood up to your father where you and your brother were concerned. I should have insisted you and Lucy marry when we learned of the baby." She dabbed her eyes again and turned to Lucy. "How will you ever forgive me?"

"There's nothing to forgive," Lucy replied softly. "All we can do is try to make the best of what we have now."

The following Sunday Loretta was in a nervous tizzy. Scott's brother, Mike, had invited everybody over for Sunday dinner at the Bufford estate, and Loretta was certain she would end up doing something to embarrass Lucy.

"Don't be ridiculous," Lucy said. "I'm proud of you. Anybody would be thrilled to have you for their mother." Each day she was becoming more proud. As Loretta's health improved, she became more optimistic about life and took greater care with her appearance. Her self-confidence was improving.

"You'll help me pick out something to wear?" Loretta said with the eagerness of a schoolgirl. "I don't have anything fancy."

"A simple dress will do," Lucy told her. While she

looked through her mother's closet for something presentable, she was dismayed to find most of what she owned was rather worn. She remembered how nervous she herself had been the first time Scott had invited her to his parents' home for dinner. She'd worn her best outfit.

Lucy pulled out a jade-green dress she'd seen her mother wear to church. "This should do nicely," she said. "I think I have a scarf that will jazz it up a bit." She decided once Loretta lost a few more pounds they'd go shopping.

"Will Scott's mother be there?" Loretta asked, pulling a pair of scuffed beige pumps from her closet.

Lucy nodded. "Don't worry about her," she said. "She feels bad about everything and will probably go out of her way to be nice."

By the time Scott and Jeff arrived, everybody was dressed and ready to go. "You girls look terrific," Scott said, opening the car door for Loretta, who insisted on sitting in the back with Kelly and Jeff.

Lucy could hear her mother fidgeting with her purse in the backseat and knew she was anxious about making a good impression on Scott's family. She wondered if one of the reasons Loretta was so nervous was that she was employed by the Buffords and had spent much of her life working on a production line. She decided, despite her own anxiety, she would do everything possible to make her mother feel comfortable. Still, she felt her heart flutter when they pulled up in front of the Bufford estate.

The mansion itself was lovely, a massive three-story stone structure surrounded by gardens. A sweet-looking collie stood near the front steps and wagged her tail. "This is Lady," Jeff said, petting the dog affectionately. "Her manners are better than Pepper's."

Scott's brother, Mike, met them at the door and hugged Lucy tightly the minute he saw her. She had always been fond of Mike, who'd covered for her and Scott after Aubrey had forbade them to see each other. "Welcome back, Lucy," he said. "We've missed you. He nodded a hello to Loretta, then paused and looked at Kelly. "And this must be my new niece," he said, insisting he get a hug from her as well. "Scott's told me all about you. Come inside and meet Becky and the kids."

As they entered the large foyer, Lucy noted the house still looked imposing with its marble floor and freestanding stairs. She smiled when she found a tricycle parked inside the door. Mike smiled as well. "Mother thinks we're crazy for letting the kids ride their toys in here," he said with a chuckle, "but I figure, what's a house for if you can't enjoy it?"

They found Naomi and Becky sitting in the formal living room with a freckle-faced boy and girl who hurried to the door the minute they spotted their cousin Jeff. Scott made the introductions, first presenting his mother to Loretta. Naomi, tucked inside her wheelchair, nodded regally. Scott moved on to Becky, a slender woman wearing a long braid down her back, who invited them all to sit.

"Excuse the toys," she said. "I just picked up in here twenty minutes ago, and the little brats have already pulled everything out again."

"There's a perfectly fine nursery upstairs," Naomi replied. "I don't know why you insist on allowing the children to take over the entire household."

Becky smiled at her mother-in-law in such a way that it was obvious they'd had the discussion before. "Now, Mother, you know how I feel. A house is not a home without children and pets."

As Lucy took a seat next to her mother, she was relieved to see the changes that'd been made in the living room. The walls and drapes had been dark before, the furniture consisting mostly of rare antiques that Lucy had been afraid to touch. It had reminded her of a museum. Now the room was bright and cheerful, from the multicolored Chinese needlepoint rug to the plump floral sofas and club chairs. Fresh flowers adorned every table, and the old prints depicting dogs at a hunt had been replaced with bright scenes. A large orange tabby cat slept on his back in front of the fireplace and didn't so much as twitch when the guests arrived. As Becky introduced their children, including their four-month-old son, Lucy could feel her mother relaxing a bit.

A chubby woman peeked in and asked Becky if she was ready for the hors d'oeuvres. "First, come meet everybody," she said, motioning the shy woman into the room. "This is Alma, our housekeeper and cook. Actually, we consider her part of the family. She's been cooking all day, and I have to admit the smells from the kitchen have been tempting."

Alma preened under Becky's praise and nodded at the newcomers as they were introduced. "I'll get the snacks, ma'am," she said. She hurried out of the room, and Mike offered refreshments from a wet bar tucked behind a folding door while the women took turns holding the baby. All in all, it was a noisy group but a happy one. Even Naomi smiled from time to time as her grandchildren played at her feet.

Jeff and Kelly looked uncomfortable with all the commotion. "Uncle Mike, is it okay if I show Kelly the stables?" the boy asked.

Mike grinned. "Just as long as you promise not to

take her up in the hayloft. That's where your daddy and me used to take all the pretty girls."

Naomi sniffed. "Really, Michael, must you be vulgar? After all, they're related."

"I'm only kidding, Mama," Mike said. "Go ahead, Jeff. But don't stay too long, Alma will have dinner ready soon."

The teenagers looked relieved to be on their own for a while. Becky excused herself, stating she wanted to put the baby down, and carried him from the room. By the time she returned, Mike and Scott were in the midst of a funny story about something that had happened at one of the plants recently. Before long, they had Loretta, who'd spent twenty-five years in a citrus plant, chuckling and adding stories of her own.

Jeff and Kelly returned, and Alma announced dinner. The group filed into the formal dining room behind Scott, who was pushing Naomi in her chair. Becky insisted Naomi sit at the far end of the table next to her eldest son. As Lucy took her place next to her mother, she noted the room's stark decor had been softened with floral place mats, fresh flowers, and bright watercolors. The chairs, which she remembered had been covered in a burgundy velvet at one time, had been redone in a gay print.

"I like what you've done to the house," Lucy whispered to Becky. "It's so homey."

Becky, in the process of seating her two children on either side of her, looked pleased. "It was a job, let me tell you," she responded, keeping her voice low so Naomi couldn't hear.

Alma carried in a silver tray of soup bowls containing a light but delicious consommé. Lucy noted her mother watched everyone else before selecting utensils. Afterward, they were served a Caesar salad and, finally, the main dish, beef Wellington with new potatoes and fresh asparagus.

"Everything is delicious," Loretta told Alma when she arrived with the dessert tray. The woman nodded and set a baked apple with vanilla ice cream before her. "Why, this is what Lucy fixes us at home," Loretta said.

Lucy smiled. "Becky called me to see if there were any foods you couldn't eat, and I asked her to go light on the dessert."

"What had you been planning to serve?" Loretta asked her hostess.

Becky grinned. "Pecan pie."

Loretta's hands flew to her chest as though she feared her heart would stop beating. "Oh, my favorite."

The group laughed. Alma poured coffee and disappeared once more into the kitchen. Jeff and Kelly excused themselves to watch television in the den, while the adults conversed and chuckled as the little ones yawned and fidgeted at the table. Alma returned and offered to take the children upstairs and get them into their pajamas so Becky could stay with her guests.

"I don't know why you refuse to hire a nanny," Naomi told her daughter-in-law once Alma had led the children away.

"I love being a mother," Becky said. "Besides, Alma doesn't mind helping out with the kids once in a while."

"How do you expect to socialize with your husband?" Naomi asked.

Mike looked at his wife and smiled warmly. "Becky and I don't do much socializing right now, Mama. We figure our children are small only once, and we'd like to spend as much time as we can with them."

Naomi sniffed. "Well, you boys had a nanny, and the

two of you turned out perfectly fine." She looked at Lucy. "What do you think, dear?" she said. "Do you think it was wrong of me to hire a nanny for my boys?"

Lucy, in the process of sipping her coffee, paused and wished the woman had not decided to pull her into the conversation. "Wrong?" she said. "Of course not, Mrs. Bufford. You had your way of raising children, and now Becky has hers. That doesn't make either of you right or wrong. Just different in how you do things."

Becky winked at her. Naomi seemed to consider her answer.

Loretta shifted in her chair. "I'm sure all mothers have their own opinions of how they'd like to raise their children," she said, talking slowly as though choosing her words carefully.

Lucy smiled proudly at her mother. As self-conscious as Loretta was about being there, she had tried to jump to her daughter's defense. Lucy was sure it hadn't been easy.

"I suppose," Naomi said at last. "I must appear inflexible at times to my family, but I find the older I get, the harder it is to bend to new ways."

"I know what you mean," Loretta said. "I'm getting quite set in my ways as well."

Naomi looked amused. "Do you find you have little rituals for everything you do?" she asked.

Loretta nodded. "First thing I do when I get up in the morning is turn the TV to the *Gospel Hour* and grab my coffee and newspaper. I don't want to talk to anybody till I'm on my second cup, and I've read 'Dear Abby' and 'Hints from Heloise.' And I can't go to bed at night unless I watch David Letterman's monologue. I don't give a flip about his guests, just got to hear his jokes. Puts me in a good frame of mind for bedtime." As though suddenly realizing she'd said a mouthful, Loretta glanced around and clamped her mouth shut.

Naomi chuckled and nodded as though she could relate to everything Loretta had said. "I drive the staff at Restful Valley crazy with my little rituals," she confessed. "They all know I do it for attention—just ask Lucy."

It was still early when Scott pulled up in front of Amy's house to drop Jeff home. For the first time, Lucy got to see where Amy lived. The house was picture perfect, the lawn and flower beds well maintained. Several lights burned from the windows, giving the place a cozy, lived-in look. Jeff had said good-night and climbed out of the car, promising to see them soon.

They pulled into Loretta's drive some minutes later. Loretta, obviously suspecting Scott and Lucy wanted to be alone for a while, suggested they go for a drive. She and Kelly were looking forward to watching a movie together, she claimed.

"What movie, Grandma?" Kelly asked, drawing smiles from Lucy and Scott as she climbed out of the car with her grandmother.

"I'll tell you about it once we get inside," Loretta said. "C'mon now, let's not tarry."

Scott grinned at Lucy in the front seat. "Sounds like a pretty good movie," he said. "You want to watch it at my place?"

Lucy suspected they wouldn't go anywhere near the television set if they went to Scott's house. Not that she'd mind. Since the night they'd made love after the dinner at Barefoot Bubba's Barbecue, they'd looked for ways to be alone. They couldn't seem to get enough of each other, couldn't stop touching or kissing. Lucy had not realized how starved she'd been for affection. She realized he was waiting for her answer. "Let's go, handsome."

Scott made the drive to his house in record time. He began undressing Lucy the minute he closed and locked the front door behind them. Their mouths fused together hungrily as he carried her into the bedroom wearing only her bra and panties.

Scott had to force himself to take it slow once they were completely undressed. He kissed Lucy deeply; he had never forgotten the flavors and textures of her mouth. He kissed her eyelids, her ears, and pressed his lips against the hollow of her throat, where he felt her rapid pulse. He kissed her breasts, her navel, the musky-scented place between her thighs, and tongued her until she climaxed.

They were both ready by the time he entered her, and Scott realized their lovemaking couldn't have been more flawlessly choreographed. Their bodies blended and moved in perfect unison. It was erotic and beautiful. Afterward, Scott held her close.

"I have only one question for you," he said when his breathing had returned to normal.

Lucy smiled sleepily, content to snuggle against his big, warm body. She hated the thought of having to dress and go home. "What is it?" she asked.

"Will you marry me?"

She had not been prepared for that; in fact, she hadn't even seen it coming. "Run that by me again, please."

"Marry me, Lucy. I know we're about fifteen years late, but I aim to make up for it."

She was so stunned by the proposal that she blinked several times at the ceiling. Finally, she sat up and pushed her hair from her face. "I don't know what to say," she replied, feeling all trembly and flustered.

Still lying on his pillow, Scott studied her from behind; her gently sloping shoulders, the flawless skin, the curve of her waist and the flaring of hips. "Surely you're not surprised," he said. "I mean, where else would we go from here? We love each other. We were meant to be together."

"Yes, but so much has happened. What about Kelly and Jeff?" She wanted to add Amy's name to her list but didn't.

"They'll be happy for us."

"I don't know, Scott. This is a big step."

"For you, maybe, but not for me." He noted her thoughtful look. "Why are you hesitating, Luce? I'm thrilled at the idea of us being together. I thought you would be too."

"Of course I'm happy," she said quickly. "I just want to make sure you've thought this through clearly. I don't want you to feel pressured because of Kelly."

He reached for her, pulling her down beside him. "Have you any doubts about how I feel?"

His body was warm and clean-smelling, with only a hint of the aftershave he used. In just a short time she had learned how to give him the most pleasure, and he had reciprocated in ways that made her blush when Alice caught her daydreaming about it at work. She thought of him constantly, found herself smiling like a goofy, love-struck teenager when he showed up unannounced to take her to lunch. God, she had fallen head over heels in love with him all over again.

"Earth to Lucy," Scott said, noting she was still deep in thought.

She saw the uncertainty in his face and knew he was

waiting for her answer. Such a big man, she thought. Not to mention powerful and self-assured. It pleased her to know he could be vulnerable where she was concerned. "The offer indeed sounds promising, Mr. Bufford," she said, fluttering her eyelids. "Perhaps what I need is a little more convincing on your part."

Scott surprised her by grabbing both wrists and pinning her to the bed. "You just bought yourself a whole lot of trouble, lady."

NINE

The wedding, which took place two weeks later, was supposed to be small and intimate, but quickly got out of hand once Loretta and Naomi took control. The little Baptist church was overflowing the day Scott and Lucy exchanged vows. Afterward, Mike and Becky held the reception at the Bufford estate. Amy attended with Jeff and sat on the groom's side, a smile plastered to her face. It was impossible for Lucy to tell whether the woman was truly happy for them, but she refused to let herself dwell on it and ruin the happiest day of her life.

"You looked beautiful today, Mom," Kelly told Lucy as she helped her out of the cream-colored linen coat dress she'd been married in. "I'm going to miss you while you're gone."

Lucy hugged her daughter tight, trying to blink back the tears that had threatened to fall for the last two days. She and Scott hadn't spent ten minutes together in the past thirty-six hours with all they had needed to do. Never in her wildest dreams would she have believed it possible to plan such an event in fourteen days, and now that it was over, Lucy simply wanted to go to bed. "I'm only going to be gone a week," she told Kelly. "I'll call you and Grandma every night."

"You don't have to do that," Kelly said. "It's your honeymoon."

Lucy hung up her wedding dress. Although Loretta had wanted her to go all-out with satin and lace, she'd selected something more practical. Now she slipped into a comfortable smoky blue skirt and short-sleeved tunic that she would wear on the plane. "You'll help Grandma stay on her diet?"

Kelly nodded, then frowned. "You know she's probably out there stuffing her face right now."

Lucy laughed. "I'll allow her this one day. Tomorrow I expect her to be back on the program."

Joining their guests once more, Lucy tossed her bridal bouquet, and Alice Bloom almost trampled the women next to her as she snatched it. No one would ever have guessed that Lucy had thrown it in Amy's direction.

Scott and Lucy told their guests good-bye and hurried, beneath a shower of birdseed, toward the white limousine parked in front of the estate. Scott waved, Lucy threw kisses, and a moment later they were on their way. Scott raised the window, and Lucy collapsed against the plush seat.

Scott grinned as he reached for the bottle of champagne that had already been uncorked and chilled in a bucket of ice. "You look like one of those inflatable dolls that just lost all her air." He reached for a tulip-shaped glass nearby. "Champagne?"

"Just give me the bottle," she said. She took a long swig before passing it back to him.

He looked amused as he raised the bottle to his lips. "That bad, huh?"

"We should have eloped."

"Your mother would never have forgiven us."

Lucy leaned against his shoulder. He felt so strong, so solid. He was hers. She tried to absorb it all as they drove to the small airport where Scott kept his plane.

There was much hand-shaking and back-slapping when they arrived at the airport, which consisted of a tiny waiting room and rest rooms. Lucy was introduced to Scott's pilot, Luther Conrad, an older, neatly dressed man who seemed genuinely happy for them. Although Lucy was a bit nervous at the prospect of flying in the single-engine Cessna, Luther quickly assured her the flight would be a good one.

Scott decided Luther must have convinced her, because shortly after takeoff, Lucy drifted to sleep and didn't wake up until they approached the airport in Jamaica.

Their hotel was pale pink and sprawling and nicer than anything Lucy had ever stayed in before. The honeymoon suite was fabulous, boasting a sitting room, a king-sized bed, a large marble Jacuzzi, and a wet bar complete with a stocked refrigerator. Noting how tired Lucy still looked, Scott ordered room service. She ate very little before falling asleep in her slip.

She awoke in the morning to sunshine and Scott leaning over her, watching her sleep. "Good morning, Mrs. Bufford," he said.

She blushed and tried to hide it by stretching. "How long have you been watching me?"

"Long enough to know you snore."

"I do not!"

"Take my word for it. We may have to sleep in separate bedrooms."

Finally feeling rested after all the hullabaloo of their

wedding, she reached up and curled her arms around his neck, then brought his face down for a kiss. "Once I get finished with you, mister, you'll think twice about separate bedrooms."

He kissed her gently, gathering her up in his arms. She was warm, her body still flushed from sleep. Her slip had scooted up and showed plenty of long, shapely leg. He stroked her calves and thighs and marveled at their smoothness.

"Uh, Scott?"

He was in the process of nibbling her earlobe. "Yes, babe?"

"I feel sort of gritty."

He chuckled. "I've already run your bath, madam." He scooped her up and carried her into the marble bathroom. She was delighted to see the tub filled with bubble bath and a tray with coffee, rolls, and fruit beside it. "Pinch me," she said. "I know this must be a dream."

She sank into the hot, sudsy water a few minutes later, oohing and aahing her delight. Scott, wearing silk boxers, had draped a napkin over one arm. "Coffee, madam?" he said, filling a delicate china cup.

"Yes, please."

He prepared it the way she liked it and handed it to her. "Anything else?"

She giggled. "Yes, I want you to feed me grapes and speak French to me."

Scott chuckled. "But, madam, I do not know French. However, I can still recall a few curse words from my college Spanish courses."

"That'll do, Raffe."

"Raffe?"

"That *is* your name?"

He sat on the edge of the tub, picked up a grape, and

popped it into her mouth. "Yes, Raffe Bandito, at your service, señora." As he fed her another grape, he mumbled a few more words in Spanish.

Lucy suddenly looked indignant. Without warning, she pulled him into the tub, silk boxers and all. Scott came up sputtering. "What'd you do that for?"

"You forget, I had two years of Spanish in high school, buster," she quipped. "You just called me a donkey."

He looked surprised. "That's not what I said."

She crossed her arms and gave him a speculative look. "Then what'd you say?"

"I said, where I come from I'd have to pay your father one hundred donkeys for your hand in marriage. That's a lot of donkeys, señora."

"Oh." She sniffed. "Well, then. That's better."

Scott stood and pulled off his boxers, and Lucy felt her stomach clench at the sight of her naked husband. They spent the next hour sipping the fragrant coffee and washing each other. Lucy took absolute delight in rubbing her hands over Scott's chest, his powerful thigh muscles, his sturdy calves and feet. He was beautiful, and he was hers. She swelled with pride. When it was his turn to wash her, she marveled that his big hands were capable of such gentleness.

Before long, they were both eager for lovemaking. They climbed from the tub and dried each other before returning to their bedroom. Their lovemaking was slow and thorough. Scott tasted her with thanksgiving. As he moved over her, their gazes locked. He entered her, and their sighs rose up like music.

The next few days passed with lazy abandon. They dozed and ate and made love. At times, they ventured out of their room to bask in the sun and listen to the music of a reggae band. In the evening they took long walks on the beach, holding hands, talking about issues that ranged from important to insignificant to downright silly.

By the middle of the week, Lucy had tanned a dark apricot. Scott became so aroused at the sight of her oiled body in a bathing suit that he couldn't contain himself. They hurried back to their suite and made love with the taste of sweat and suntan oil on their skin.

They shopped and lunched at quaint restaurants, talking for hours under whirring ceiling fans. Lucy noted that Scott excluded Amy from much of his conversations of the past, and she was thankful. Truthfully, though, she no longer felt insecure about his previous relationships. She had only to look at him to know where his heart belonged.

On the last day, Scott ordered coffee and Danish to be brought up to the room, and as they sipped their first cup, he and Lucy discussed their immediate future.

"It's up to you," he said. "We can live in the lake house or build something."

She'd already made up her mind she wanted to live in the lake house, and she told him as much. "It's plenty big enough. If we decide to have more children, we can always add on."

"Speaking of children," Scott said. "We haven't always taken precautions. Would it bother you if you got pregnant right away?"

She was thoughtful. "I suppose not, although I wouldn't mind having you all to myself the first year or two. What about you? How do you feel?"

He shrugged. "Hey, I'm open. We can start making babies right away as far as I'm concerned."

She laughed. It occurred to her that she had never

been so happy. She sighed wistfully. "I wish we didn't have to go back so soon."

He pulled her close and tucked her head beneath his chin. "Just because we go home doesn't mean the honeymoon has to be over," he said.

She thought of his parents and her parents, neither of whom had been happily married. "That's what all couples say. But you just wait, before long we'll be taking each other for granted, and all the zip will have gone out of our lovemaking."

He cupped her chin and tipped her head back so that she was looking directly into his eyes. "You don't believe that any more than I do."

She felt her breath catch at the intensity of his gaze. She couldn't imagine ever looking at him and not thinking how lucky she was to have him. Still, it was hard to feel optimistic when she considered the divorce rate. "What makes you think we'll be any different from other married people?" she asked.

"Because we waited fifteen years for this, Lucy. If our love can survive something like that, it can survive anything."

They arrived home the following evening, bearing gifts. Loretta and Kelly held a private party for them. The hors d'oeuvres consisted of miniature tuna fish sandwiches, low-fat cheese and crackers, stuffed cherry tomatoes, and fruit. Kelly and her grandmother opened their gifts while Lucy told them all about their trip.

"I'm so happy for you, I could spit," Loretta said, hugging Lucy tight.

"Have you stuck to your diet?" Lucy asked.

"Yes, daughter. I've lost a total of twelve pounds.

Now, can we stop worrying about that and concentrate on your new marriage? I can tell it suits you, you're absolutely glowing!" She hugged Scott. "You've made my daughter very happy, and for that I thank you."

His eyes were warm as they locked with Lucy's. "She's made me pretty happy too," he said.

They left a short time later. Lucy was tired from their trip and wanted to soak in a hot tub. "Do you think Loretta will be okay?" Scott asked. "She looked a bit sad as we pulled away."

Lucy smiled. "She'll miss us at first, but I think she'll be glad to have the house to herself again. It's not easy with three females living in cramped quarters."

They arrived home, and Kelly hurried into her new bedroom to unpack, leaving Scott and Lucy at the door. He grinned and set the luggage down, then swept Lucy high in his arms and carried her over the threshold. He kissed her lightly on the lips before setting her down. "Welcome home, Mrs. Bufford," he said.

"I'm glad to be here," she replied.

Lucy could feel her expression turning goofier by the minute, her smile widening, growing sloppy. She knew part of it was due to fatigue, but in all honesty, the man only had to look at her these days for her to become goo-goo eyed. Scott, feeling rather silly himself, shoved his hands in his pockets and glanced around the room.

"The place is sort of plain," he said. "Feel free to decorate it as you like."

She let her eyes roam over him. "I'd say it's decorated just fine."

He cocked his head to the side, amused. "Are you flirting with me, little lady?"

Kelly picked that particular moment to walk into the room. "Mom, remember when Scott said I could decorate my room—" She paused, glancing from her mother to her father. "Oh, jeez," she mumbled. "I should have known it was going to be like this. This probably isn't a good time to tell you I want to paint my bedroom black."

Lucy glanced at her daughter. "Did you say something, honey?"

"Um, I just wanted to make sure it was okay with you if I went ahead and ordered the paint for my room."

Lucy nodded, but her eyes never left Scott's face. "Sure. Let me know if you need any help."

Scott pulled Lucy into his arms and nipped an earlobe. "I'll make a deal with you," he said. "I'll bring the luggage in and start unpacking if you'll run us a hot bath."

Later, as Lucy lay beside Scott and listened to his gentle breathing, she decided it felt good to be home.

The following Monday came much too quickly for the new family, who had not yet adjusted to their routine. Lucy arrived at Restful Valley, where Naomi greeted her with a big hug, and the staff held a party, complete with naughty gag gifts. Alice wept out of sheer happiness.

Lucy arrived home that day to find Scott cooking dinner and Loretta sipping iced tea as she prepared a salad. "Hi, honey," her mother said. "I stopped by to drop off a few more wedding gifts, and Scott invited me for dinner. Hope you don't mind."

"Of course not," Lucy said, greeting her new husband with a brief kiss. "Why would I?"

"I just thought the two of you would appreciate some time alone."

Scott chuckled. "We have a teenager on the premises, remember?"

"Kelly is always welcome at my place," Loretta said.

Lucy shared a secret smile with Scott. "Thanks, Mom. We may take you up on that from time to time."

Lucy prepared a glass of iced tea for herself and opened the wedding gifts, showing them to Loretta, who recorded each one so Lucy could send thank-you cards.

"Oh, this one's from Amy and Jeff," she said, tearing into a box wrapped in white paper. She peered at it. "Flannel sheets?"

"Let me see," Loretta said, hurrying over to look. "Hmm. I know people use them up north, where the winters are unusually cold, but I can't imagine it getting that cold in Florida."

Scott was only vaguely aware of what they were saying as he studied the recipe before him, a spicy hot jambalaya that he'd wanted to try for weeks. At one time he hadn't been able to boil water. Once he'd learned to cook, he'd looked at it as sort of a hobby, and Lucy was only too happy to let him take over in the kitchen. In return, she cleaned up.

"Maybe Amy thinks I'm not woman enough to keep my husband warm on cold nights," Lucy blurted out.

Loretta almost choked on her iced tea.

Scott looked up at her tone of voice. "What?" He chuckled. "Well, we both know that's not true. I'll be sure to set Amy straight the next time I see her." He went back to reading his recipe.

"I hope you're not serious," Lucy said.

He gave her a blank look. "Huh?"

"I think I'll go see what Kelly's up to," Loretta said, hurrying out.

Scott put down the recipe and stepped closer to his

wife. "I'm sorry, babe, I wasn't paying attention. What'd you say?"

"I said I hope you aren't serious about sharing our bedroom habits with your ex-wife."

He was completely baffled. "Why would I?" He glanced down at the opened gift. "Are you upset over the fact Amy sent us flannel sheets?" he said, trying to understand what had her miffed. "If you don't like them, send them back."

"I can't do that."

"Then give them to your mother. Maybe she can use them."

"She doesn't have a king-sized bed."

Scott threw his arms out in frustration. "I don't care *what* you do with them, Luce. Throw them in the trash."

"Don't you want to read the card that came with the gift?" she asked testily.

"Should I?"

"It concerns you. It seems Amy and Jeff are planning a little party for us this Friday night. She's invited all your old neighbors."

He dropped his hands to his sides. "I wish she hadn't done that."

"That makes two of us."

"I'll just call her and tell her we can't make it."

"You can't do that. She's probably already mailed out the invitations."

"Then what do you propose I do?" he asked.

Lucy sighed and sat down at the table. "I don't care. Just answer this one question. How does Amy know you have a king-sized bed?"

He studied her blankly. "She's seen the house before, Lucy. She even offered to decorate it for me, but I told her I liked it the way it was. Why are we fighting over something this silly?"

"We're not fighting. And it's *not* silly."

Scott regarded her. She'd been so moody the past couple of days, he was certain she was still worn out from their wedding and honeymoon. Everything had happened so fast, he'd learned firsthand the meaning of whirlwind.

He walked over to her chair and got down on his haunches. "Listen, babe, we'll do whatever you want. I'm sure this is Amy's way of showing us how happy she is for us. I don't think she would have done it if she'd known it would make you uncomfortable."

Lucy wasn't so sure. "We can go," she said dully, already worrying about what she would wear, how she would act. If only she didn't feel so run down, but Scott had a habit of waking her during the night for lovemaking. Of course, it didn't matter what time he woke her, her body was always ready for his touch. At times it seemed she couldn't get enough of him.

Scott noted the dark circles under her eyes and felt like a jerk. Here she was, having to get up early for work each morning, and he couldn't seem to keep his hands off her at night. How selfish could he be? He took her hand and kissed it. "You look exhausted," he said. "I'm going to sleep in the guest room tonight so you can get your rest."

"I don't want you to sleep in another bed," she protested.

He stood. "I insist. It's the only way I know you'll get a good night's sleep. Once you're rested, I'll rejoin you." He knew it was the only way. All he had to do was rub against her during the night, and his body went hot all over.

Lucy tried to hide her hurt as he walked over to the stove and went about preparing his dish. She reached for the phone book and looked up Amy's number, then went to the phone and dialed. "Hello, Amy?" she said the minute the other woman answered. "This is Lucy. Scott and I are thrilled over the party you and Jeff are throwing for us. What time shall we be there?"

It was the longest night of her life, and when Lucy awoke the next morning, she felt sick to her stomach from having spent so much time worrying.

It pained her to think Scott preferred sleeping alone to sleeping with his new wife, and the only reason she could come up with was their argument over Amy's party. Was she just being jealous and petty where Scott's ex-wife was concerned?

Perhaps the woman *was* merely trying to welcome her into their lives. Besides, Scott had made it plain many times before that he respected Amy and planned to maintain an amicable relationship with her because of Jeff. What else could Lucy expect him to do? How would she ever respect him if he turned his back on his son and ex-wife?

Lucy told herself to face facts. Amy was going to be around for the rest of their lives. She and Scott would share in every one of Jeff's achievements. As his wife, Lucy would be able to share in those events as well, but if she made it hard on Scott, he wouldn't welcome her being there. She had to come to terms with the fact that Amy was going to be around no matter what. They were all going to grow old together. Lucy could accept it or spend the rest of her life being miserable.

First things first, though, she told herself. She had to get Scott back in their bedroom as soon as possible.

He looked as handsome as ever when he carried her coffee in and put it on the night table. He took one look at her and frowned. "Are you feeling okay?" he said, noting how pale she was.

"Fine," she mumbled. "I think all that spicy food got to me last night."

"I probably put too much cayenne pepper in the jambalaya," he said. "I keep forgetting, not everyone craves hot food like I do. Can I get you something? An antacid? A glass of milk?"

"No, I'll be okay once I've had my coffee."

He sat on the edge of the bed and took her hands in his. "I missed you last night."

"You were the one who insisted on sleeping in the guest room."

"I did it because I thought you needed your rest. I've had a perpetual hard-on since you came back into my life."

She leaned over and kissed him. "I'd be disappointed if you didn't."

He pulled her into his arms and held her. "How about lunch today?"

"As long as you promise to visit your mother for a little while. She claims you never have time for her since you married me."

"Okay, I'll drop by half an hour early, how's that?"

Lucy nodded and reached for her coffee, then took a sip. It tasted funny. "Did you put sugar in it?"

He nodded. "Of course I did."

Kelly knocked on the bedroom door and peered in. "I'm leaving now."

"How are you getting to school?" Lucy asked, since she usually dropped her off on her way to work.

"One of the editors from the school paper is picking me up. I volunteered for the job because you said I should get involved, remember?"

"Boy or girl?" Lucy asked.

"He's a senior. But he's not my type, and this is not a date. So don't worry."

"You could have mentioned it at dinner."

"You were . . . preoccupied. It's no big deal, Mom. We won't end up in Mexico living in sin, okay?" She closed the door.

Lucy shook her head. "I'll worry the rest of the day."

"She's growing up, babe. You're going to have to learn to let go."

"Easy for you to say. But I know how poor your Spanish is. If she *does* end up in Mexico, we're in trouble." Lucy glanced at the alarm clock. "I'd better get my shower."

"Want me to join you, señora?"

She smiled. "That would be nice, Señor Bandito."

They stepped into the warm spray a moment later and Scott helped her wash her hair, then he soaped her from shoulder to toe, spending extra time on her breasts and thighs. She in turn washed him, grinning wickedly at the sight of his erection. "You're one hot tamale this morning," she teased. They dried quickly and ended up in bed, where they made love in record time.

Afterward they dressed, kissed, and hurried away to their jobs.

Lucy arrived to find her patients just returning from breakfast. Naomi stopped her in the hall and looked up from her wheelchair. "Well, did you ask my son when he's going to visit?" she demanded.

Lucy smiled. "Today, as a matter of fact. If you like, I'll help you with your hair as soon as I get a few things squared away out here."

Naomi's look softened. "That would be nice, thank you."

They met in Naomi's room a few minutes later, once Lucy had seen that all was as it should be. As she started brushing the woman's hair, Naomi met her gaze in the mirror.

"You're frowning. What's wrong?"

"I'm just concerned about several of our patients."

"Who?"

"Oh, I probably shouldn't discuss it with you."

"I don't see why not. I know everything that goes on around here."

Lucy sighed. "A few of our patients don't even bother to get out of their chairs all day," she said. "It's all we can do to get them out of bed."

"Yes, well, you can't force people to do something they don't want to do."

"I'm afraid they're going to wither away. If only I could *motivate* them, encourage them to take walks or do a few stretching exercises, know what I mean? I just don't have time to do it myself."

"We had an aerobics teacher here for a while," Naomi replied, "but nobody could keep up with her. Some of the nurse's aides tried to get an exercise program going, but they didn't have much success either. Frankly, I thought the whole thing rather absurd. One girl tried to get us to do jumping jacks, of all things. Can you imagine people in their seventies and eighties doing jumping jacks, for heaven's sake? Why, it's a wonder somebody didn't get hurt."

Lucy looked thoughtful. "What we require is someone who understands the needs of senior citizens," she said. "Someone who's graceful and elegant and can show these people how to move to soft music in such a way that won't cause injury. Also, this person should be an organizer of sorts."

Naomi pursed her lips and met Lucy's gaze in the mirror. "Young lady, you don't fool me for a minute. You've been looking at my file, haven't you?"

"Your file?" Lucy said innocently.

"You know darn well I studied dance for fifteen years as a girl, and you also know that as Aubrey Bufford's wife, I served on more committees and fund-raisers than anyone else in this town."

"You don't say."

Naomi sighed. "I'm pleased as punch that you would consider me for this position," she said, "and you know I wouldn't expect a dime for it. But I'm afraid with my crippling arthritis—"

"Naomi?"

"Yes, dear?"

"We both know you don't have crippling arthritis, now, don't we?"

The woman gasped. "How can you say that? Why, I'm eaten up with it!"

"You will be if you don't get out of that chair and start moving around. Now, I'd appreciate it if you'd think about this little job offer. Restful Valley has several vans at your disposal; we'll be glad to go along with whatever outings or other social events you can think of. I have every confidence you'll come up with something exciting. There now, I think your hair turned out rather nicely, but I still think something short would be chic." She left the woman sitting in her wheelchair, utterly speechless.

Lucy was in the process of going through a client's chart, when she heard a chorus of whistles and cat calls. She glanced out her office in time to see Scott walk in. He closed the door and leaned against it as though he feared for his life.

"These people may be elderly, but they still have dirty minds," he said.

Lucy chuckled as she planted a kiss on his mouth. "Oh, well, I guess that's to be expected, seeing as how we're newlyweds and all."

"You feeling any better?" he said.

"I'm fine. Now, be a good boy and go visit your mother. I still have to get a few things out of the way before I can go to lunch."

Scott exited just as Alice stepped through. They chatted briefly before he left to find Naomi. Alice sighed dreamily.

"If I had a hunk like that, I would never get out of bed."

Lucy chuckled. "You don't have to convince me he's handsome."

"Obviously not. You look exhausted. Isn't he letting you get *any* sleep?"

Lucy blushed. "I think I'm coming down with a bug. The past few mornings I've had to literally force myself out of bed, and my stomach feels queasy."

"Maybe you're pregnant."

Lucy laughed, then sobered instantly. "Oh, my, I hadn't thought of that."

"Are you using birth control?"

"Sometimes. Not always."

"When was your last period?"

Lucy tried to think. Some nurse she was, she thought to herself. She'd been so caught up with wedding and honeymoon plans and starting a new life that she couldn't remember.

"Well? You know what they call people who *sometimes but not always* use birth control, don't you?"

"What?"

"Parents."

"Hmmm."

"You'd better buy yourself one of those home pregnancy kits."

Lucy didn't mention her conversation with Alice to Scott over lunch. Instead, she found herself on the defensive concerning Naomi.

"My mother thinks you're not taking her ailments seriously," he said once they'd ordered sandwiches in a quaint little deli within a short drive from Restful Valley.

"She's right. She has no business being in that wheelchair, and I have every intention of getting her out of it."

Scott studied her. "I don't mean this to sound critical or anything, but as long as her bills are paid, why should it matter?"

"The more she relies on other people to help her, the less she'll do for herself. If she's going to remain in Restful Valley, I'd like to see her contribute to those whose health problems are more serious.

"You realize she'll be helping herself as well," Lucy said when Scott didn't look convinced.

"How?"

"Did you know many elderly patients are on some form of antidepressant?" she asked.

"I'm not surprised. Getting old is a depressing subject."

"It doesn't have to be. Sure, there are more aches and

pains and health problems, but if people just sit around thinking about them all the time, of course they're going to be down in the dumps. I don't expect our clients to play tennis or run around a track, but they can swim and bowl and go to the movies. I'm sure they'd love to go on an outing once in a while, perhaps to St. Augustine to visit the Fountain of Youth."

"That costs money, you know," Scott pointed out.

"Restful Valley can afford it. Besides, even if the board of directors balk at spending the money, our clients are more than capable of paying their own way."

"So where does my mother fit in?"

"Who would be better at organizing these events?"

Scott smiled. "Well, if you can get her involved, then I'm all for it."

Their food arrived, and they ate in silence for a moment. It wasn't until Scott had finished his meal that he told Lucy he had to go out of town.

"For how long?" she asked, trying to hide her disappointment.

"One night, maybe two. One of our plants north of here is having serious personnel problems. I'd ask you to come with me if I thought you could get off work."

"When do you have to leave?"

"Today. Luther says we've got bad weather on the way, so he wants to get the trip behind us as soon as possible."

"I second that motion," she said, knowing she'd worry if he had to fly through thunderstorms. "Just hurry back. I've sort of gotten used to having you around."

Scott drove her back to Restful Valley, and they shared a long kiss before Lucy climbed out of the car. She went inside, where she found plenty to keep her busy for the rest of the day, but she couldn't shake the feeling of gloom that had settled over her as soon as Scott had announced he was going out of town.

Finally, she told herself she was being silly. She could spend the time with her mother and daughter.

Lucy left work at five-thirty, after having called her mother to invite her to dinner that night. On her way home she stopped by the drugstore and purchased a pregnancy kit, then picked up a pack of chicken breasts at the supermarket. She arrived home and found Kelly doing her homework at the kitchen table.

"Hi, sweetie, how was your day?" she asked, putting the small sack containing the pregnancy kit under the sink and out of sight.

The girl shrugged. "Okay, I guess. Some redneck tried to get my phone number, but I told him my mother only allowed me to date boys who bathed on a regular basis and still had their own teeth."

"Oh, Kelly, what a thing to say."

"I hate this place, Mom. I have no friends—"

"You have Jeff and the friends you've met through him."

"Yeah, but his mother's acting kinda weird since she found out I was his half sister."

"Weird? Like how?"

"Like maybe she doesn't want us to get too close now that she knows we're related. I guess she's afraid we'll fall in love, get married, and have a bunch of deformed kids."

Lucy knew her daughter sometimes exaggerated. "Do you know this for a fact, or is it something you've just convinced yourself of?"

"Ask Jeff, he'll tell you. He was going to invite me to go horseback riding with him and his friends last weekend, but his mother asked him not to. Naturally, he told me."

Lucy was still thinking about Kelly's problem when Loretta arrived some minutes later bearing a tossed salad. They hugged. "What's the matter, honey?" she said. "I thought new brides were supposed to shine."

Lucy shrugged as she put the chicken breasts on a broiler pan and slid it into the oven to bake. "I'm missing Scott, I suppose. And Kelly just gave me a bit of unsettling news."

Loretta took a seat at the table next to her granddaughter. "What is it?" she asked.

Kelly repeated what she told her mother. "Jeff has already introduced me to all his friends," the girl said. "If I'm not supposed to have anything to do with him, then that means I won't be hanging around his friends either."

Loretta looked at Lucy. "You'll have to get Scott to talk to Amy," she said. "I'm sure once he explains that Jeff and Kelly are friends and nothing more, she'll change her mind."

Kelly didn't look convinced. "I'm ready to go back to Atlanta."

"You'd leave me?" Loretta cried in horror.

Kelly smiled. "No, I'd take you with me."

They ate dinner, then cleaned the kitchen together before Kelly went to her room to finish her homework. As Lucy wiped the table and chairs, Loretta began cleaning the sink. "Where's your cleanser?" she asked, checking under the sink and pulling out the small sack Lucy had hidden there. "Oh, my. I hope this isn't Kelly's."

Lucy glanced up and found her mother holding the pregnancy kit. "Of course it's not Kelly's," she said, crossing the room and snatching it from her mother's hand. "Can't I have any secrets in this house?"

Kelly walked into the room, and Lucy shoved the box back into the paper sack. She and her mother stood there, smiling stiffly at the girl. "Have you seen my pencil sharpener?" Kelly asked, then grinned. "What are you doing?"

Lucy looked surprised. "Me? Oh, nothing."

"You're hiding something in that bag. What is it?" She reached for the bag, but Lucy held it high over her head.

"It's personal," Lucy said.

Kelly giggled. "I don't care, I want to see."

Lucy tossed the bag to Loretta, but Kelly caught it in midair and glanced inside. "What on earth are *you* doing with a pregnancy test?"

Lucy's face flamed. "Well, I, uh."

Kelly stared at her mother as though seeing her for the first time. "You're *pregnant*?" she asked, her voice squeaky.

"Would you be upset if I were?" Lucy asked.

Kelly looked thoughtful. "I don't know. I guess not. Have you taken the test yet?"

"No. I was waiting until Scott returned."

"Now, Lucy, you can't expect us to wait two whole days," Loretta said. "I'll go crazy."

"Grandma's right," Kelly said. "Besides, Daddy wouldn't be upset with you for telling us first."

Lucy hedged. "I think the father should be the first to know."

"He's going to call you tonight, isn't he?" Loretta asked.

Lucy nodded. "He said he'd call around eight."

"Okay, that's thirty minutes from now. You can take the test, then wait until he calls to make the announcement."

Lucy nodded. "That sounds fair." She started out of the room, and they followed. She came to an abrupt halt. Her mother and daughter bumped into her. "Where do you think you two are going?" she said.

"We just thought we'd wait outside the bathroom door," Loretta said.

"No way," Lucy told them. "You're both going to wait right here. Kelly, find the deck of cards. We'll play gin rummy till your father calls."

Lucy was gone less than ten minutes. When she returned, she found Loretta and Kelly at the kitchen table. They studied her intently. But if they hoped to glean something from her expression, they were wrong; Lucy's face was unreadable. She sat down at the table and regarded her daughter coolly. "Okay, deal the cards."

They played in almost dead silence, speaking only when it was absolutely necessary. "It's eight o'clock," Loretta said. "Why hasn't he called?"

"He'll call," Lucy replied.

At eight-fifteen the phone rang, startling them so badly, they jumped. Lucy got up to answer it. "Oh, Scott, it's you. Hi, honey."

"Tell him," Loretta ordered.

Lucy waved her off. "Scott, I'm afraid I have some bad news," she said, drawing frowns from her mother and daughter. "You know that room you keep your weights in? Well, you're going to have to move them out so we can add a nursery."

"Yes!" Kelly and her grandmother gave each other a high-five.

On the other end of the line, Scott was stunned. "You're pregnant?" he said.

"Do you mind?" she asked.

His voice was husky when he spoke. "I'll show you how much I mind when I get home," he said. By the time he hung up, Scott realized he was trembling. And smiling like a lovestruck teenager. They were going to have a baby! Oh, but life was grand.

TEN

Loretta had just pulled out of the driveway, when the phone rang. Lucy hurried to it, thinking it might be Scott. Amy spoke from the other end. "Lucy, is that you?" she said.

Lucy chuckled. "Who else would it be, Amy?"

The woman sighed. "Oh, sorry, I'm not thinking straight. Is Scott there?"

"No. Is something wrong?"

The woman on the other end of the line hesitated. "I know you're going to think this is silly, but my bathroom toilet won't stop running. It kept me up half the night last night."

"Did you call a plumber?"

"Yes, but he can't come for a couple of days. I'll never be able to get up for work tomorrow if I don't get a good night's sleep. I wouldn't have imposed, but Scott's so good at this sort of thing."

"Yes, well, he's probably had a lot of experience," Lucy replied, knowing Amy had always called him for every little thing. She glanced at the clock and saw that it was still early. "Why don't I drive out and have a look?" she suggested.

"*You?*"

"Believe me, I've repaired my share of running toilets," Lucy said. "I'll be there in fifteen minutes." She hung up and hurried to the closet for her coat, yelling to Kelly that she'd be out for a little while.

When she arrived at Amy's, a surprised Jeff answered the door. "Hi, Lucy," he said. "What in the world are you doing here?" He glanced past her. "Is Kelly with you?"

"No, I—"

"Jeff, please don't keep Lucy standing out in the cold," Amy said. "Invite her in."

He blushed. "I'm sorry. I was just surprised to see you." He stepped back and held the door open for her.

Lucy saw that Amy was already in her bathrobe. "If you'll just show me which toilet is giving you trouble, I'll be glad to take a look."

Jeff glanced at his mother. "You asked Lucy to fix our toilet?" he said. "Why didn't you tell *me*? I would have looked at it."

"Since when did you become a plumber?" Amy asked her son.

"I'm not. But neither is Lucy."

As they bantered between themselves, Lucy took a moment to study her surroundings. The house had been done in a country motif with frilly curtains and overstuffed furniture covered in quilted fabric. Baskets and dried flowers hung from the ceiling and knickknacks covered every conceivable space. "Your home is lovely," she told Amy, although in all honesty she was feeling a little claustrophobic.

Amy smiled proudly. "Thank you. I'm quite happy with it. Follow me," she added politely.

The country look was repeated in the master bedroom and bath. Lucy noted the toilet was indeed running annoyingly. First, you'll need to clear off the top of the tank so I can look inside," she said, although she suspected she already knew what the problem was. Amy moved several baskets of potpourri and bath soaps aside so Lucy could remove the lid from the tank. She peered inside.

"Hmmm. Just as I thought."

"What is it?" Amy said, peering over as well.

"Your chain broke in half."

"Is that bad?"

"Not bad enough to call a plumber. Do you have a paper clip?"

"Sure." Amy hurried away. She returned a moment later. "I brought two just in case."

"Okay, let me show you how this is done," Lucy said. "In case it happens again. See these ends?"

"Yes."

"I'm just going to connect the two with this paper clip—" She paused. "Like so." She glanced up. "You're going to have to replace the chain, of course, because it's corroded. You can buy them in any hardware store."

Amy looked impressed. "Where did you learn to do this?"

Lucy put the lid back on the tank. "I bought a couple of books on plumbing and repairs. I could never afford to hire someone to do the work for me."

Amy looked slightly amused. "And you didn't have an ex-husband you could call on."

Lucy smiled also. "Well, no."

Amy looked thoughtful. "Would you mind lending me the books?"

Lucy tried to mask her pleasure. "I'll drop them off tomorrow."

Lucy awoke two mornings later to heavy rain. She had been walking on clouds since she'd discovered she was pregnant, and she refused to let the bad weather dampen her spirits. What fun it would be planning for the event, choosing a doctor, preparing the nursery. Naturally, she would ask Scott to be in the delivery room with her. And this time, when she left the hospital, Scott would be by her side. They would share the joys of parenting which they hadn't been afforded after Kelly's birth.

Lucy climbed from her bed and made her way into the kitchen. She poured a cup of coffee and switched on the little TV set next to the sink. She turned the dials until she found the weather channel. The storm Scott had mentioned had turned into a tropical depression during the night and was expected to make landfall by late afternoon. As she listened, a storm advisory beeped across the bottom of the screen.

Kelly stumbled in a few minutes later and found her there.

"What are you watching?" the girl asked sleepily.

"The weather. We're supposed to have thunderstorms all day."

"Yuck."

"Your dad's flying home this afternoon. I'm worried."

Kelly shrugged. "I'm sure his pilot knows what he's doing," she said. "By the way, why didn't you tell me you were going to Jeff's last night? He called and said you were trying to repair Amy's toilet. I think he was embarrassed she'd called you instead of asking him."

"Perhaps next time she won't need to call *anyone*," Lucy said.

"Also, Jeff had a long talk with her, said he liked the idea of having a sister, and she apologized to him for trying to keep us apart."

"That's good news," Lucy said. She hadn't wanted to bring the matter up with Amy until she'd had a chance to discuss it with Scott. Now she was glad that wouldn't be necessary.

The weather hadn't improved by the time Lucy arrived for work. She literally ran into Alice in the hall. Alice had been out the day before, attending a meeting in Miami. She grabbed Lucy's hand and pulled her into her office.

"Well? Did you buy one of those kits?"

"The test was positive."

Alice squealed and hugged her. "Congratulations!" she cried. "I'm so happy for you. Have you told Naomi yet?"

"No, I just got here," she said, indicating her raincoat. They were interrupted by a brief knock on her door. Lucy opened it and found Naomi Bufford standing on the other side, a sheaf of papers in one hand, an ivory cane in the other. Her hair had been cut in a short but flattering look.

She almost gasped. "Naomi, you're—"

"Standing," the woman replied haughtily. She stepped into Lucy's office. "I hope you don't mind the cane, my dear, but one can't go directly from a wheelchair to playing hopscotch in the hallway."

Lucy tried to suppress a smile. "Well, I know how

determined you are, Naomi. You'll toss that cane away in no time." She motioned to the papers in her hand. "Are those for me?"

"Yes. I jotted down a few ideas on how I could help motivate these people, as you suggested. I've also called various tourist agencies, and they promised to send me information."

Lucy noted Alice's blank look. "Naomi's going to be our new activities coordinator," she said.

"It's strictly volunteer work," Naomi replied. "I certainly don't want people to think I need the money."

"Oh, how wonderful," Alice said. "You're perfect for the job."

Naomi preened. "Yes, well, I suggest we get started as soon as possible. I've asked Becky, my daughter-in-law, to pick up a few cassettes for me, Frank Sinatra and Glenn Miller tunes as well as a few classical pieces for the exercise classes."

"Exercise?" Alice looked worried now.

"Nothing harsh," Lucy said hurriedly. "Just simple stretch routines to music."

"I'll need someone to type this notice and put it on the bulletin board so we can begin next Monday," Naomi said. "I plan to call my group the Swinging Seniors. Catchy, huh?" She handed a slip of paper to Alice, who promised to see to it right away.

"Thank you, Naomi," Lucy said. "I know you won't regret it."

"Why didn't you tell her about the baby?" Alice said as soon as the older woman had left them.

Lucy shrugged. "I think it'd be better if Scott and I told her together."

Alice left and Lucy was finally alone with her thoughts. By lunchtime, the weather had worsened. Lucy decided to grab a salad from the kitchen instead of going out. By four o'clock, the thunder jolted through the building, and the power was knocked out twice. Shortly before five, Lucy called the Shade Tree Citrus Plant to see if Scott's secretary had heard from him.

"I just spoke to him ten minutes ago," the woman said. "He was on his way to the airport. They should land in Shade Tree around six."

"In this weather?" Lucy asked anxiously.

"I'm sure the pilot won't take any unnecessary risks," the secretary said. "But I wouldn't want to be the one flying in this weather."

Lucy thanked her and hung up. The anxiety she'd been feeling all day had settled like a lead weight in the pit of her stomach. Without saying good-bye to anyone, she grabbed her purse and left.

Scott paced the Dade City, Florida, airport as he waited for his pilot to file their flight plan. Finally, Luther Conrad hurried toward him. "If you're still wanting to leave, we'd best go now," he said.

Scott saw through the large plate glass windows that the storm that had begun late the night before hadn't let up.

"They're going to let us take off in this?" he asked Luther.

Luther nodded. "As long as we've got a half mile of visibility," he said. "But in another fifteen minutes we might not have it."

"Is it safe?"

"I've flown in better," Luther said, then shrugged. "But I've flown in worse too. You, uh, seem to be in a hurry to get back."

Scott studied the man before him, who had more than thirty years' flying experience under his belt. There wasn't anyone he trusted in the cockpit more than Luther.

"I guess I *am* in a hurry," Scott replied after a moment. "I recently found out I'm going to be a father."

A big grin split Luther's usually reserved face. "Then, what are we waiting for?"

Fifteen minutes later, they were up. Scott had belted himself into the passenger seat of the Cessna and was already going through paperwork in his briefcase. They bumped for a few minutes. "How's it going up there, Luther?" he asked without looking up from his work.

"It's a big storm," the pilot said. "If I try to go around it, we might end up in Memphis. I'll try to pick out the soft spots. Just don't take off your seat belt."

Lucy muttered colorful words under her breath as she waited for the snarl of traffic to start moving. The rain pelted her windshield, making it impossible to see more than a couple of car lengths in front. She did see flashing lights ahead and suspected there'd been an accident. There was only one road leading to the airport, and she was on it.

Scott decided if he'd ever had a tendency to get airsick, now would have been the time. The flight was as bumpy as a carnival ride. He wanted to ask Luther if everything was okay, but he didn't want to break the pilot's concentration. He knew they weren't far from Shade Tree now. All he could think of was getting on the ground, getting home to Lucy.

At five minutes of six, Lucy pulled into the small airport and parked beside the building. The parking lot was empty of cars, the offices and hangar deserted. Rain came down in torrents, the wind was fierce and gusting. She grabbed her umbrella and climbed from the car, but a gust of wind hit her so hard, she was flattened momentarily against the building. A few minutes later, she thought she heard a plane's engine.

Scott had put his briefcase aside after it had fallen from his lap twice, scattering papers across the aisle. Finally, Luther announced their approach to the landing strip in Shade Tree.

"Looks like everybody's gone home already," he said. "I'll just have to take her down on my own. Keep your fingers crossed, we've got wind coming from every direction."

Scott leaned back in his seat and closed his eyes, feeling weary after his business trip but tense over the flight. He should never have insisted Luther bring him home in such weather. Not only had he risked his own safety, he was risking that of his pilot's. All he could think of was getting home. Home to Lucy.

He felt the plane descending, knew Luther was coming in for a landing. Glancing out his window, he could see the runway ahead of them. Then, a second later, the plane touched down and bounced several times before veering sharply to the left.

"Damn crosswind," Luther muttered. "The right landing gear's broke."

Scott wanted to ask him what that meant, but the plane suddenly went into a wild ground loop.

Scott braced himself, expecting the worst.

He felt the plane skid, knew the second they'd left the runway. Lights flickered, then died, leaving him in semi-darkness. The cabin pitched violently, and the plane flipped completely over, jarring him from head to toe as the sound of twisting metal echoed in his ears.

In horror, Lucy watched the whole thing. She heard a shrill scream and realized it had come from her. The plane came to an abrupt halt, belly-up like a dead insect, in the drainage ditch that ran beside the runway. Scott was dead. They'd been given a second chance, only to lose it.

Lucy saw the pay phone nearby. She ran to it and dialed 911. "There's been a plane crash!" she blurted out. "The airstrip on highway eleven." She dropped the phone, kicked off her heels, and ran, fast as she could, down the runway. Luckily the wind was at her back, propelling her forward. She winced as she stepped on something sharp, but kept on running.

"Luther, are you okay?" Scott asked, trying to unbuckle his seat belt. He and the pilot were both hanging upside down.

"Yeah," Luther called back. "You?"

"I don't think anything's broken."

The pilot crawled from the cockpit and made for the door. Scott noticed a small cut over one eyebrow.

"Let's get out of here in case it catches fire," Luther said.

Lucy was less than fifty yards from the plane when she saw the door swing open. Two men, one of them Scott, stepped onto the wing and jumped. They climbed from the ditch and hurried away from the aircraft.

She couldn't believe her eyes. "Scott!" she cried at the top of her lungs.

Scott glanced up at the sound of his name and saw Lucy closing in on him fast. "Lucy, what on earth—"

She literally threw herself at him, eager to feel his solid body against hers. "You're alive!" she exclaimed.

"What are you doing out here?" he demanded, noting she was drenched and shivering from the cold rain.

Lucy was only vaguely aware of Luther. She glanced toward him and saw blood trickling down his face. Her legs turned to rubber.

Scott saw her sinking to the ground and caught her. He noted her feet, clawed and scratched and bleeding from running barefoot. "It's okay, Lucy, it's okay," he said, lifting her and cradling her in his arms as he would a child.

Her relief turned to anger. "Damn you, Scott Bufford!" she yelled. "Why did you put me through that? You could have died. You could have—" She buried her face against his chest and sobbed. In the distance, there was the sound of approaching sirens.

Lucy cried nonstop on the way to the hospital while Scott tried to calm her. Luther had been taken away in another ambulance.

"She'll be okay," the paramedic said, tucking a blanket around her trembling body. "She had a bad scare, that's all."

The ambulance came to a screeching halt outside emergency, and Lucy was whisked in on a stretcher. Scott suddenly found himself surrounded by doctors and nurses. "I'm fine," he said. "Please see to my wife."

They were released two hours later, once the wounds on Lucy's feet were cleaned and dressed and Luther's eyebrow stitched. Loretta and Kelly had brought dry clothes, as had Luther's wife. Lucy joined her mother and daughter in the lobby. She felt drained, and her feet hurt. "Please take me to your place," she said.

Loretta looked surprised. "*My* place? But what about Scott?"

Lucy's eyes teared. "Please don't ask me a lot of questions right now, Mother. I just want to go home."

Scott stepped into the lobby a few minutes later after having consulted with the doctor who'd examined Lucy and learning she was okay. There was absolutely no reason to suspect a problem with the baby. He glanced around now, expecting to see Lucy with her mother and Kelly; instead he found himself surrounded by strangers. He hurried over to the receiving desk.

"Have you seen my wife?" he asked the woman who'd checked them in upon arrival.

"She just left, sir," the woman said. "I believe her mother took her home."

Scott sped home and was as much surprised as he was disappointed to find the driveway empty. Where had Loretta taken Lucy, he wondered, hurrying inside the house. He dialed Loretta's number, and the woman answered after several rings.

"Is Lucy with you?" he asked, feeling frantic.

Loretta hesitated. "Yes. She asked me to bring her here."

He sighed his relief. "Okay, I'll be right there."

"Don't come right now, Scott," Loretta said. "Lucy doesn't want to see you."

He couldn't believe his ears. "Doesn't want to see me?"

"She's still very upset over the plane accident. Naturally, the doctors couldn't give her anything to calm her down because of the baby. She's resting now, thank goodness. I think it'd be best if she slept here tonight." She paused. "I'm sorry, Scott."

"But, Loretta—"

"I have to go now."

The click in his ear made him jump.

After three days of sniffing and sneezing due to the cold she'd caught standing in all that rain, Lucy climbed out of bed. Although the cuts and bruises on her feet were healing nicely, they were still tender. She stood there, trying to decide what she was going to do with her life. Luckily, a tap on the door prevented her from having to make an immediate decision. Loretta peeked in.

"Oh, you're awake," she said brightly. "Look, more flowers." She handed Lucy a long, narrow box. "They must be from Scott. He's the only one who sends roses."

Lucy read the attached card, another apology from her husband and a request to visit. She glanced around her already crowded bedroom. Mike and Becky had sent a bright bouquet the day before, Alice and Naomi a potted plant. Even Amy had called to check on her the day after the crash, to let her know the party had been postponed until she was up and around. Scott had sent a dozen yellow long-stemmed roses every day. "Put them in your room," Lucy said. "I'm beginning to feel like I'm in a hospital."

"Scott's called twice already. He wants you to call him back."

"Yes, well, he can keep on waiting," she mumbled.

Loretta looked sad. "Honey, you can't be mad at him forever."

Lucy looked at her. "I'm not mad," she said. "I'm hurt. Unbelievably so."

"It's not his fault the plane crashed."

Lucy sighed. "Mother, do you have any idea what I went through watching that plane go down? And it was

Scott's stupidity for insisting that the pilot make the flight to begin with."

"He was just in a hurry to see you, sweetheart. He was excited about the baby."

Lucy felt the sting of tears. "I know he was. But what good would it have done either of us if he'd died? This is the second time I've gone through something like this with him. I just can't go through life not knowing what to expect."

"Life is full of risks, Lucy," Loretta said. "Maybe if I'd taken a few more when I was young, you and I wouldn't have spent our lives living with a mean drunk."

An hour later, there was another tap at her bedroom door. Lucy had finally pulled on some clothes and brushed her hair, but she was no closer to feeling like her old self than before. "Come in, Mom," she said.

The door opened and Scott stepped through. "Hi," he said softly.

Lucy stared at him for a full minute. "What are you doing here?" she demanded.

He closed the door behind him. "You and I need to talk. I'm not leaving until we do."

"I have nothing to say to you."

He stepped closer. "So you're going to leave me because I made one silly mistake?"

"One silly mistake?" she said. "Is that what you call it? Well, it almost cost you your life, not to mention your pilot's. And what about me, Scott? Did it ever cross your mind *even once* what it would have done to me if you'd died in that crash? I've already raised one baby by myself."

"We'd been cleared for takeoff, Lucy. Luther told me himself."

"Maybe so. But I seriously doubt he would have landed in a deserted airport in that kind of weather unless you'd insisted."

"Luther has flown for over half his life, Lucy. Pilots fly into noncontrolled airports all the time. He had no way of knowing the crosswinds were so severe that day. These things happen sometimes. Luckily, we were able to walk away from it."

"Maybe this time," she said. "But what about next time?"

"There won't be a next time. I won't ever ask him to take a chance like that again. I was just impatient this time, but I think you know the reason for that."

Until now, Lucy had avoided looking directly into his eyes. She gazed into them now and saw her own emotions mirrored there. "Scott—" She paused when her voice trembled. "You have no idea what I went through when I thought I'd lost you the first time. I was so scared, so unsure of myself—" She paused again as tears sprang to her eyes. "So lonely."

"Baby, please don't do this to yourself."

"I have to. I have to make you understand. Living with Darnel was so bad. I never wanted you to know just how bad it was. He never had a kind word to say to me, and he was always putting me down. My mother told me to ignore him, but it wasn't easy. I grew up thinking I was a nothing and a nobody."

"You weren't any of those things, Lucy. You were the brightest, prettiest girl at Shade Tree High."

"Only because you made me feel good about myself, Scott. But then, when I thought you were dead and I was all alone in Atlanta, all those insecurities started coming back. I almost didn't go to nursing school because I didn't think I could do it. I'd spent my entire life listening to Darnel tell me how stupid I was.

"What I'm trying to say is, I had to look deep inside myself for the courage. I knew your father's money wouldn't last forever. It was up to me to make a good life for Kelly. It was up to me to find the self-confidence to do these things."

Scott walked over to the bed and sat down. "And you did it by telling yourself you didn't need anybody." He looked at her. "Am I right?"

"Yes."

"And that's why you're afraid to need me now?"

She nodded. "It all came rushing back to me as I watched that plane flip over with you in it. I realized I had already begun to need you again, and I was going to have to start completely over."

Scott took her hand. "If I *had* died in that crash the other day, what do you think would have happened to you?"

"I don't know."

"Yes, you do, Lucy. First of all, you and Kelly and the baby would be set for life financially. I've already seen to that. As for whether or not you would have been able to go on, you know as well as I do that you're more than capable of taking care of yourself and our children. You would have grieved over my death, but it wouldn't have destroyed you."

She pondered it. Maybe she was stronger than she thought. "You and I were forced to grow up fast," she said.

"But you especially, Lucy," he said gently. "I had friends and a family. You had no one. But look what you did with your life. You should be very proud.

"I want you to need me, Luce," he added. "Because I've always needed you. I don't think that makes me a weak person."

"I just don't want you to think of me as one of those clinging-vine types," Lucy said. "I don't want to smother you."

"You mean like Amy?" He chuckled. "Jeff told me you lent her a book on home repair, and she's been poring over it ever since. She also just started dating a friend of mine from the hospital, so maybe things will work out for them." He thought of Jim Burke, the administrator, who spent all his evenings alone with a book, and he was glad the two were seeing each other.

"That just leaves us, Lucy. Please come back."

He looked so handsome that he almost took her breath away. She had loved him for as long as she could remember and would spend the rest of her life loving him. Her mother was right, life *was* full of risks, but without them how could people grow and learn to appreciate the good things that life handed them as well? And what was wrong with needing a man, when he needed her just as much? She would simply have to toss her hat in the ring and take a chance the way everybody else did, because life would be meaningless without Scott.

"I'm ready," she said. "Let's go home."

THE EDITORS' CORNER

Summer must eventually come to an end, but romance never has to. In fact, next month LOVE-SWEPT brings you a heat wave of exciting, passionate tales that are just perfect for warding off the end-of-the-summer blues. Keep that iced drink handy!

Fayrene Preston's acclaimed DAMARON MARK series continues with **THE DAMARON MARK: THE SINNER,** LOVESWEPT #798. Sinclair Damaron hates himself for inspiring the fear that darkens Jillian Wythe's gray eyes as he lures her into his trap. Then Jillian awakens in a world of tropical beauty and is shocked to discover she wants Sin as much as her freedom! But a fever of revenge has the entire Damaron clan in its grip, and Jillian learns that Sin intends to use her as bait. An explosive story of danger and desire, dark sensuality and reckless romance—from #1 bestselling author Fayrene Preston.

Attraction sizzles on every page as Laura Taylor blends heartbreaking emotion and risky passion in **FALLEN ANGEL,** LOVESWEPT #799. When Thomas Coltrane's new next-door neighbor insists she wants him to keep his distance, he can't agree less. From her husky voice to her expressive hands that speak in sign language, Geneva Talmadge is one tantalizing challenge he's never faced before—in a courtroom or a bedroom. And he isn't about to let a little thing like her cool treatment of him stop him from winning her love. Award winner Laura Taylor has created a one-of-a-kind courtship that makes for nonstop reading.

Please welcome talented newcomer RaeAnne Thayne and her wildly romantic debut, **THE MATING GAME,** LOVESWEPT #800. Chase Samuelson is still the most gorgeous male Carly Jacobs has ever known. She's never forgotten her teenage crush on him or his betrayal years before, but now he's back and the chemistry between them is more combustible than ever. She'd given Chase her heart, trusted him with her dreams. Is his return her second chance to taste the fire of his kiss? Chase and Carly's bittersweet reunion is part genuinely touching, part brashly funny—and 100 percent wonderful. Look for more RaeAnne Thayne novels in the months to come.

Fresh from her triumphant THE THREE MUSKETEERS trilogy, Donna Kauffman now takes us on a journey through Cajun mysteries with **BAYOU HEAT,** LOVESWEPT #801. Though naked and bloodied in her bathtub, Teague Comeaux gives Dr. Erin McClure a smile wicked enough to charm a lady out of her clothes! She'd asked for a guide into voo-doo country, but Teague looks like trouble. And when he escorts her right into the middle of danger and intrigue, she's certain he's the devil in disguise. Donna Kauffman weaves dark seduction into every page of this steamy, spellbinding romance.

Happy reading!

With warmest wishes,

Beth de Guzman

Shauna Summers

Beth de Guzman   Shauna Summers
Senior Editor   Editor

P.S. Watch for these Bantam women's fiction titles coming next month: Rising star Susan Krinard returns to the land of the bestselling PRINCE OF WOLVES with **PRINCE OF SHADOWS**. And in **WALKING RAIN**, Susan Wade makes a stunning debut that showcases her disarmingly original style and deft supernatural touches. And immediately following this page, preview the Bantam women's fiction titles on sale *now*!

Treat yourself to

MISCHIEF

the newest hardcover by *New York Times*
bestselling author

Amanda Quick

*To help her foil a ruthless fortune hunter, Imogen
Waterstone needs a man.
Not just any man, but Matthias Marshall,
the intrepid explorer known as
"Coldblooded Colchester."*

"You pass yourself off as a man of action, but
now it seems that you are not that sort of man at
all," Imogen told Matthias.

"I do not pass myself off as anything but
what I am, you exasperating little—"

"Apparently you write fiction rather than
fact, sir. Bad enough that I thought you to be a
clever, resourceful gentleman given to feats of
daring. I have also been laboring under the
equally mistaken assumption that you are a man
who would put matters of honor ahead of petty
considerations of inconvenience."

"Are you calling my honor as well as my
manhood into question?"

"Why shouldn't I? You are clearly indebted

to me, sir, yet you obviously wish to avoid making payment on that debt."

"I was indebted to your uncle, not to you."

"I have explained to you that I inherited the debt," she retorted.

Matthias took another gliding step into the grim chamber. "Miss Waterstone, you try my patience."

"I would not dream of doing so," she said, her voice dangerously sweet. "I have concluded that you will not do at all as an associate in my scheme. I hereby release you from your promise. Begone, sir."

"Bloody hell, woman. You are not going to get rid of me so easily." Matthias crossed the remaining distance between them with two long strides and clamped his hands around her shoulders.

Touching her was a mistake. Anger metamorphosed into desire in the wink of an eye.

For an instant he could not move. His insides seemed to have been seized by a powerful fist. Matthias tried to breathe, but Imogen's scent filled his head, clouding his brain. He looked down into the bottomless depths of her blue-green eyes and wondered if he would drown. He opened his mouth to conclude the argument with a suitably repressive remark, but the words died in his throat.

The outrage vanished from Imogen's gaze. It was replaced by sudden concern. "My lord? Is something wrong?"

"Yes." It was all he could do to get the word past his teeth.

"What is it?" She began to look alarmed. "Are you ill?"

"Quite possibly."

"Good heavens. I had not realized. That no doubt explains your odd behavior."

"No doubt."

"Would you care to lie down on the bed for a few minutes?"

"I do not think that would be a wise move at this juncture." She was so soft. He could feel the warmth of her skin through the sleeves of her prim, practical gown. He realized that he longed to discover if she made love with the same impassioned spirit she displayed in an argument. He forced himself to remove his hands from her shoulders. "We had best finish this discussion at some other time."

"Nonsense," she said bracingly. "I do not believe in putting matters off, my lord."

Matthias shut his eyes for the space of two or three seconds and took a deep breath. When he lifted his lashes he saw that Imogen was watching him with a fascinated expression. "Miss Waterstone," he began with grim determination. "I am trying to employ reason here."

"You're going to help me, aren't you?" She started to smile.

"I beg your pardon?"

"You've changed your mind, haven't you? Your sense of honor has won out." Her eyes glowed. "Thank you, my lord. I knew you would assist me in my plans." She gave him an approving little pat on the arm. "And you must not concern yourself with the other matter."

"What other matter?"

"Why, your lack of direct experience with bold feats and daring adventure. I quite understand. You need not be embarrassed by the fact that you are not a man of action, sir."

"Miss Waterstone—"

"Not everyone can be an intrepid sort, after all," she continued blithely. "You need have no fear. If anything dangerous occurs in the course of my scheme, I shall deal with it."

"The very thought of you taking charge of a dangerous situation is enough to freeze the marrow in my bones."

"Obviously you suffer from a certain weakness of the nerves. But we shall contrive to muddle through. Try not to succumb to the terrors of the imagination, my lord. I know you must be extremely anxious about what lies ahead, but I assure you, I will be at your side every step of the way."

"Will you, indeed?" He felt dazed.

"I shall protect you." Without any warning, Imogen put her arms around him and gave him what was no doubt meant to be a quick, reassuring hug.

The tattered leash Matthias was using to hold on to his self-control snapped. Before Imogen could pull away, he wrapped her close.

"Sir?" Her eyes widened with surprise.

"The only aspect of this situation that truly alarms me, Miss Waterstone," he said roughly, "is the question of who will protect me from you?"

RAVEN AND THE COWBOY
by Sandra Chastain

"An extremely talented author whose writing
is . . . warm and real and lovely."
—*New York Times* bestselling author
Heather Graham

*He first came to her in a dream: a sleek and tawny
cougar with the power to protect her. So when Raven
Alexander awoke to find herself lying beside the rug-
ged stranger, she wasn't afraid. He might be an un-
ruly cowboy with a checkered past but Raven believed
the spirit guides had sent him to help her find the
sacred Arapaho treasure.*

It was the sound of thunder that woke Tucker,
followed by hard, pelting rain that stung his face.
He sat up, disoriented for a moment as he tried
to remember where he was.

Rain. He was outside. But where was Yank? A
flash of lightning lit up the sky, revealing the side
of the cliff and an opening in the rock before
him. He pushed himself onto his elbows, his head
vibrating as if he'd been hit by the lightning
flashing in the distance.

Gingerly he began to feel his way toward the
wall, his hand encountering something in the

darkness—something that ought not to be there. An ankle. A slim ankle leading to a foot encased in a soft moccasin.

Tucker froze. He wasn't alone. Wherever on the west side of hell he was, he had a woman with him. But why wasn't she having a reaction to his touch? Another jagged streak of silver split the sky and illuminated her face—he could see that she was an Indian, wearing a buckskin dress.

He must have had more to drink than he'd thought. Maybe he was hallucinating. Or this was a dream. No, the leg he held was real. It was warm and soft and feminine. But something was wrong. No woman would sleep through a storm.

The rain came down harder. If he didn't get the woman out of this downpour, she'd get sick. Taking her by the arm, he tugged her against him. With one hand behind him and the other arm around her waist, he inched away from the edge.

At last, with one final jerk, they were inside the cave, out of the elements. Tucker shivered from being wet. His bedroll was on Yank's back, wherever Yank was. Tucker didn't want to think that the horse had gone over the edge with him. Tucker always took care of his horse. Just like his namesakes, the big black was indestructible. They were a good match, a Southern Rebel and a horse named Yank. Both were survivors.

The cave was small and damp. The woman, still lying against his chest, was cold. He shook her gently, waiting for a reaction. But the only response he felt was his own as the top of his index finger found the space beneath her breast.

"Ma'am . . . Lady . . . I beg your pardon, but would you wake up."

She moaned and turned slightly so that her face was against his chest. His hand, below her breast only moments ago, was now holding it. Tucker froze, waiting for her to come to her senses and chastise him for his liberties.

But she didn't wake. He had the absurd feeling that he'd been cut into two people. His head ached fiercely while the lower half of his body, very much alert, announced a raging male hunger. Until he understood what was happening, he'd forced his thoughts and touch away from that need as he cradled her head and laid her down.

That's when he found it, the wound, blood now dried across a deep cut in her scalp behind her ear. However she'd come to join him in this godforsaken place, she, too had come accidentally. Nobody deliberately fell off a cliff. But what was he going to do? The rain hadn't let up. It was too dark to see how to get back to the trail, and he wasn't sure he was steady enough on his feet to get them there.

If he could find some dry sticks or limbs, he could build a fire. Reluctantly he let go of her and waited for the next flash of lightning. Once he was reasonably certain that they weren't sharing the cave with any animals, he began to explore, encountering the remains of a pack rat's nest.

In the cantina he'd had tobacco and matches.

He reached into his shirt pocket, hoping they were still there. They were, along with the half-breed's gold nuggets and the watch fob. Now the bandits had another excuse for chasing him—the loot.

Shielding his meager makings of a fire from the wind, Tucker cupped his hands and struck the first match against a stone. It flared briefly, then died. There were only a few matches left. He couldn't afford to waste another.

Closing his eyes, he prayed for a moment of calm as he lit another match. This time the moss blazed up, igniting the sticks. Momentarily he had a tiny fire going.

Though meager, the fire soon warmed the air inside the small cave. Tucker sluiced water through the woman's head wound and winced at the depth of it. He didn't know why she wasn't dead. She could die still if he didn't get her warm.

Removing his sheepskin jacket, he covered her, checking beneath her wet clothing for a sign that her body temperature was rising. It wasn't. Finally, because he knew nothing else to do, he lay down beside her and pulled her against him. He didn't intend to doze off, but the heat from the fire and the woman's body soon made him drowsy.

As the storm raged outside, Tucker Farrell covered himself and the woman with his jacket. Then he did something he had never done with a woman before. He slept.

She cast a spell of passion in a
dangerous duel of hearts.

From the dazzling new talent of
Juliana Garnett
author of *The Quest*
comes a spellbinding romantic tale
for those who believe in

THE MAGIC

*Although Rhys ap Griffyn hurried back from King
Richard's crusade to claim his heritage, he met his fate
in a forest clearing, in a mysterious woman who
barred his way and set his blood afire. Wrapped in
shadows, the lady with raven-dark hair might have
been an enchanted creature, for the locals had warned
him not to ride on Beltane Eve. But Rhys didn't believe in faeries, and the exotic Sasha felt real enough
to him. . . .*

He had done no more than press his lips to
the dimple at the corner of her mouth when Rhys
heard a voice callling his name, faraway and insistent. He tried to ignore it, but the persistent
sound grew too near. Halting, he looked up with
a scowl at the interruption. It took a moment for
his surroundings to come fully into focus, then
he saw with some surprise that he was far from

the wooded pool where he'd first met her. An alder sheltered them beneath its branches, and a small burn trickled merrily by, water splashing over the rocks. A grassy meadow sloped downward from the trees.

She shifted, then laid her fingers against his cheek; her eyes glowed softly when he glanced back down at her. "I must go," she murmured. "It grows late."

He caught her hand, holding it. "Nay, wait. 'Tis only Brian. I'll send him away."

She slowly withdrew her hand and rose to her feet, and he followed reluctantly. "I cannot . . ." She cast a glance over her shoulder as Brian's voice grew louder and nearer. Gathering her cloak around her, she took a step away from him, repeating, "I must go."

He grabbed her hand again, fingers digging into her tender skin with shameless urgency. "Wait. Tell me your name and where you reside. We'll meet again once I send Brian away."

Her smile deepened as she removed her hand from his clasp and took a backward step. "Yea, we shall meet again."

He started to reach for her anew, determined not to let her go so easily, but Brian's voice made him pause. "Rhys!" came the strident call, followed by pained yowls that dwindled into rough curses directed at a clump of brambles.

Curse Brian. He glanced away, and shouted impatiently that he would be there in a moment. When he turned back, the maid was gone. Jésu— she'd been there one moment, standing near the crowded branches of flowering hawthorns, but now she was not to be seen. He looked around, dumbfounded and furious.

"Rhys," came Brian's voice again, sounding relieved and breathless as he crashed toward him through a raspberry patch. "Where have you been all day?"

"All day?" Rhys dragged his gaze away from the spot where the maid had last stood and spun to face his knight. " 'Tis but early morn. What's the matter with you? Did you not mark that I was occupied—?"

The snarled oath that accompanied this demand made Brian swallow hard. "Yea, lord," he said, looking down, "I marked it well, yet—"

"Yet you chose to ignore it." He shook his head irritably. "Now she has fled, and God only knows if I'll ever see her again."

"She?" Brian looked up from plucking a thorn from his arm, blinking rapidly. "You were with a woman, my lord?"

"Did you not say you marked it well? By all the saints, Brian, I begin to think you wine-mazed."

"Nay, lord, I've been searching for you. We thought ill had befallen you when we couldn't find you."

Rhys jerked at the ties of his loosened chausses. Damn the ache. "I went to bathe at the pond—" He broke off suddenly and looked up. "My armor and helm. I must have left them off, but I don't remember. . . ."

Brian was looking at him strangely, and Rhys

narrowed his eyes. "Why do you look at me like that?"

"We found your armor and helmet by the pool earlier." Brian swallowed heavily. " 'Tis near midday, and we despaired of finding you— you've been with her, haven't you? The Elf Queen?"

To enter the sweepstakes outlined below, you must respond by the date specified and follow all entry instructions published elsewhere in this offer.

DREAM COME TRUE SWEEPSTAKES

Sweepstakes begins 9/1/94, ends 1/15/96. To qualify for the Early Bird Prize, entry must be received by the date specified elsewhere in this offer. Winners will be selected in random drawings on 2/29/96 by an independent judging organization whose decisions are final. Early Bird winner will be selected in a separate drawing from among all qualifying entries.

Odds of winning determined by total number of entries received. Distribution not to exceed 300 million.

Estimated maximum retail value of prizes: Grand (1) $25,000 (cash alternative $20,000); First (1) $2,000; Second (1) $750; Third (50) $75; Fourth (1,000) $50; Early Bird (1) $5,000. Total prize value: $86,500.

Automobile and travel trailer must be picked up at a local dealer; all other merchandise prizes will be shipped to winners. Awarding of any prize to a minor will require written permission of parent/guardian. If a trip prize is won by a minor, s/he must be accompanied by parent/legal guardian. Trip prizes subject to availability and must be completed within 12 months of date awarded. Blackout dates may apply. Early Bird trip is on a space available basis and does not include port charges, gratuities, optional shore excursions and onboard personal purchases. Prizes are not transferable or redeemable for cash except as specified. No substitution for prizes except as necessary due to unavailability. Travel trailer and/or automobile license and registration fees are winners' responsibility as are any other incidental expenses not specified herein.

Early Bird Prize may not be offered in some presentations of this sweepstakes. Grand through third prize winners will have the option of selecting any prize offered at level won. All prizes will be awarded. Drawing will be held at 204 Center Square Road, Bridgeport, NJ 08014. Winners need not be present. For winners list (available in June, 1996), send a self-addressed, stamped envelope by 1/15/96 to: Dream Come True Winners, P.O. Box 572, Gibbstown, NJ 08027.

THE FOLLOWING APPLIES TO THE SWEEPSTAKES ABOVE:

No purchase necessary. No photocopied or mechanically reproduced entries will be accepted. Not responsible for lost, late, misdirected, damaged, incomplete, illegible, or postage-die mail. Entries become the property of sponsors and will not be returned.

Winner(s) will be notified by mail. Winner(s) may be required to sign and return an affidavit of eligibility/release within 14 days of date on notification or an alternate may be selected. Except where prohibited by law, entry constitutes permission to use of winners' names, hometowns, and likenesses for publicity without additional compensation. Void where prohibited or restricted. All federal, state, provincial, and local laws and regulations apply.

All prize values are in U.S. currency. Presentation of prizes may vary; values at a given prize level will be approximately the same. All taxes are winners' responsibility.

Canadian residents, in order to win, must first correctly answer a time-limited skill testing question administered by mail. Any litigation regarding the conduct and awarding of a prize in this publicity contest by a resident of the province of Quebec may be submitted to the Regie des loteries et courses du Quebec.

Sweepstakes is open to legal residents of the U.S., Canada, and Europe (in those areas where made available) who have received this offer.

Sweepstakes in sponsored by Ventura Associates, 1211 Avenue of the Americas, New York, NY 10036 and presented by independent businesses. Employees of these, their advertising agencies and promotional companies involved in this promotion, and their immediate families, agents, successors, and assignees shall be ineligible to participate in the promotion and shall not be eligible for any prizes covered herein. SWP 3/95

DON'T MISS THESE FABULOUS BANTAM WOMEN'S FICTION TITLES

On Sale in June

MISCHIEF

AMANDA QUICK, blockbuster author of ten consecutive *New York Times* bestsellers, dazzles with her newest hardcover. Only one man can help Imogen Waterstone foil a ruthless fortune hunter—and that's the intrepid explorer known as "Coldblooded Colchester."

_____ 09355-X $22.95/$25.95 in Canada

RAVEN AND THE COWBOY

SANDRA CHASTAIN, praised by *Affaire de Coeur* as "sinfully funny and emotionally riveting," serves up another western delight when mismatched lovers Raven Alexander and Tucker Farrell embark on a perilous quest for treasure.

_____ 56864-7 $5.99/$7.99 in Canada

THE MAGIC

A deposed heiress with the "Sight" enlists a returning Crusader's help on Beltane Eve to regain her lost kingdom, in this spellbinding tale from dazzling new talent JULIANA GARNETT.

_____ 56862-0 $5.99/$7.99 in Canada